Dear Reader:

Have you ever had your life turned upside down, with no clue as to why and how it happened? Scary thought, right? That is what makes *Duplicity* by OASIS a wonderful read. Imagine being accused of things you did not do. Imagine people claiming to know you that you have never met. Imagine your spouse becoming someone you hardly recognize. Imagine having blackouts and waking up to the police standing over you. That is what the main character of this novel has to contend with.

Motion-picture mogul Parrish Clovis is on top of the world. Married to one of the sexiest vixens alive, an Emmy-nominated actress, Parrish has it all; or so he thinks. After his face lands on the front page of every newspaper in America, accused of raping his own wife, Parrish quickly discovers that money and fame cannot shield him from the media…or the law.

A bona fide "page turner," if there ever was one, *Duplicity* is fast-paced, engaging, and full of suspense and drama. OASIS is an incredible writer with a solid literary future in front of him. Thanks for giving this novel a read and I guarantee that you will enjoy it, from cover to cover.

Thanks for supporting all of the Strebor Books authors. To find me on the web, please go to www.eroticanoir.com or join my online social network, www.planetzane.org.

Blessings,

Zane

Zane
Publisher
Strebor Books International
www.simonandschuster.com/streborbooks

ALSO BY OASIS
Push Comes to Shove

ZANE PRESENTS

Duplicity

A NOVEL

OASIS

SBI

STREBOR BOOKS

NEW YORK LONDON TORONTO SYDNEY

Strebor Books
P.O. Box 6505
Largo, MD 20792
http://www.streborbooks.com

ISBN 978-1-59309-298-6
ISBN 978-1-4391-8401-1 (e-book)
LCCN 2010925100

First Strebor Books trade paperback edition June 2010

Cover design: www.mariondesigns.com
Cover photograph: © Keith Saunders/Marion Designs

10 9 8 7 6 5 4 3 2 1

Manufactured in the United States of America

For information regarding special discounts for bulk purchases, please contact Simon & Schuster Special Sales at 1-866-506-1949 or business@simonandschuster.com

The Simon & Schuster Speakers Bureau can bring authors to your live event. For more information or to book an event, contact the Simon & Schuster Speakers Bureau at 1-866-248-3049 or visit our website at www.simonspeakers.com.

FOR...
the rhythm of your Jazz that I vibrate to.

Prologue

"When I turn thirteen," Tuesday said, "I promise to get us out of this shit hole. We're gonna go to New Jersey and find our dad." She plopped down on a filthy mattress shoved in the corner of their room.

"Don't sit down so hard." Parrish fanned the air. "Don't do that; you make all the stink come out."

"Should be used to it by now."

"I hold my breath until I fall to sleep." He looked at her with unguarded eyes and then sat beside her, careful not to disturb the odor. "I don't want to wait 'til you're thirteen." He took in their room. Yellowish newspaper covered the only window. Brown water spots stained the ceiling, identical to the human-fluid stains dotting the mattress. At least their bedroom door protected them from the chaos on the other side of it. Well...protected them until their mother found it convenient to unlock it and invite the chaos in.

"Two years ain't long. I'll protect you," Tuesday said, putting an arm around him.

"It is a long time. We might be..." The thought frightened him.

"Be what?"

"By then we could die here."

"Stop it. I won't let nothing happen to you. I always hear Catherine tell people I have a mature body for my age. When I'm thirteen, I should be able to pass for an older teenager. That way we can travel safe. We might find Daddy."

"I hate *her*." He cut his eyes at the door. "I hate 'em all."

The sound of the door being unlocked registered in their ears. Parrish's heart rattled. He started to pretend that he was someone else. Tuesday's palms slicked with sweat; her stomach knotted.

"Time to earn your keep." Catherine Dunlap stood in the threshold, swaying. She had a .32 automatic in her palsied hand, and a smoldering joint dangling from her mouth.

"I can't, Catherine," Tuesday said, lowering her gaze. "I'm still sore." She could feel that she had angered Catherine.

Catherine fired a slug into the ceiling, knocking plaster loose. "I'm your mama, goddamn it! Don't call me Catherine. Don't tell your mama no."

Parrish thought Catherine looked like a devil while a mixture of cocaine and marijuana smoke flowed from her nose. "Please, Mommy, don't make her."

She moved toward him so quick, Parrish thought she had glided across the floor. She struck him with the gun as fast as she had moved. He was stunned. Blood trickled from his scalp.

She straddled his body and put the muzzle on the blood. "You're getting a free ride. Don't nobody want a boy. How 'bout I get rid of you? Then your sister can earn her own keep."

Parrish recovered enough of his senses to see his mother's finger curled around the trigger. If there were really a God, this would be the ideal time for the Big Guy to acknowledge

Parrish's measly existence. Please, Mr. God, don't let me die. Please don't.

Tuesday tugged on her. "He didn't mean it, Catherine."

Catherine shoved Tuesday to the floor. "Bitch, I'm your fuckin' mother! Your brother is gonna die, and there's no one to blame but you. Either you earn his keep or you bury him down in the basement."

"I'm sore."

Catherine took a long draw on the joint and then pulled the trigger. Tuesday flinched when the gun made a clicking sound. Parrish, on the other hand, shit his pants.

Catherine laughed in spite of the joint and kept Parrish pent beneath her. She dug bullets from her pocket. After she loaded the clip, she pressed the gun against his forehead. "I oughta make you wear a diaper."

Tuesday covered her ears and closed her eyes. "Please. Please. Please, Catherine, they hurt me."

"Don't kill me, Mommy." His eyes flooded with tears.

"That depends on your sister." She pressed the gun harder. "Are you gonna earn his keep, Tuesday?"

"Okay," she said. "I'll do it."

"Atta girl." Catherine pulled Parrish from the mattress. "Get your pussy ass in the closet and you bet not make a sound."

Parrish took a step and his legs gave out. His head was spinning; his vision was blurred. He started crawling to the door. Instinctively, he wanted out.

Catherine kicked him in his shitty ass—hard. "Wrong door."

She locked him in the closet and turned to Tuesday. "Take your clothes off; he's waiting."

When you do not know your personal devil,
he usually manifests himself in the nearest person.
—Paulo Coehlo

Chapter 1

Parrish Clovis awoke naked on his neighbor's lawn. He was stretched out beside a mountain of Rottweiler shit. He absolutely had no idea of how he'd managed to be spooning with dog crap. He scrunched up his stubbled face at the tangy smell. He distinctly remembered climbing into bed last night and screwing his wife into a frenzy. This change of location, he couldn't explain. In fact, a lot of absurd and peculiar things had occurred lately that he couldn't explain.

He glanced at his bandaged hand. He still hadn't figured out how he'd fractured three fingers, either. One thing, though: he was grateful that daybreak was just approaching, and that his ass hadn't been busted. The thought of explaining this bout of bizarre behavior to anyone embarrassed him.

Parrish turned up his nose at the rotten stench again, pulled himself to his feet, and trudged to the fence that divided the yards, his hands covering his sacred parts. When he hurdled the fence, his wife swung open the back door of their home.

Hana looked at him with disdain. "This is absolutely

ridiculous." Her Hungarian accent was intense, match-ing her glare.

"Don't start, Hana. I'm really, really not in the mood. I smell like dog poop." He stalked by her. "I hate that dog."

"The enforcements are coming."

"You called the cops?" He sighed. "Shouldn't have done that, Han."

"My anxiety has been agitated all night." She followed him through the house. "Last time you showed up—"

"I don't need reminding."

"You swore everything was under control." She looked at the pieces of grass that clung to his brown ass. "You're nude. That's miles away from control."

He froze in his tracks and turned his head to a painting that decorated the wall of their staircase. A line creased between his brows. "Where did this come from?"

"You brought it home two days prior. Monday." Tears streaked her beautiful face. "Don't you remember?"

✪✪✪

A stolen UPS truck plowed toward its destination. Ace, the driver, was a colossus man. Six-foot-eight with a stony, pale face and hands the size of baseball mitts. He had a balding crown that peeled because of a con-stant thrashing from the sun. He smashed his size 16s against the gas pedal and put an eye on his passenger. "You are right about me; I am not a good man," the giant spoke, slow and without contractions. "It is true; I only joined the Rangers so I could kill people for free."

The passenger chuckled. "You didn't need the military. Y'all white folks been getting away with murder for centuries."

"The military was my gymnasium to practice in." Ace thumped a finger against the steering wheel. "Pop, and the enemy goes down. You are still sore that you did not beat me; could not beat me."

"I didn't kick your big ass because this trick knee gave out on me." The passenger rubbed his knee and thought back to the day Ace had taken advantage of the injury and pinned him to a mat in front of his platoon. "You don't feel good about the way you won the trophy."

"We are fifteen years away from the Rangers…Sergeant Lindsay, but it is never too late for a rematch. Fighting makes my dick hard." Ace parked curbside at an expensive home. He placed a toupee on his chapped, bald spot and patted it.

"Ace, I will fuck you up," the retired sergeant said, handing Ace a package. "Now, do what the fuck I'm paying you to do."

✪✪✪

"Two wrongs don't make it even, justify it, or make it right." Parrish shut CNN off, disgusted. "They're going to execute that brother no matter what. So what, they found him guilty? The conviction is iffy. People don't have the permission to decide who should live and who should die." He gazed through the window at his neighbor's yard and wondered about last night.

"Tookie Williams deserves the death penalty," Hana said, refilling her husband's favorite Garfield mug with coffee. "He actually did horrible things, Parrish."

"How do you really know that?" He gestured at the TV. "This thing is brainwashing you. You're becoming more and more Americanized." He said *Americanized* as if he were speaking of devil worshiping. "Trust me, Han; I know what it's like to want to be different. Before my mother died, I used to pretend I was someone else. You're Hungarian. You look Hungarian, so why do you want to feel American? Be yourself and think for yourself. Don't let the media dictate your thoughts and opinions. No human deserves to die at the hands of another human."

"I'm entitled to my opinion, of course."

"When it's yours."

"You did a great job of changing the subject. Americans are experts at deviating when they don't want to address an issue. I haven't adopted that practice."

Smart ass. He sighed. "I haven't had any symptoms since high school; I haven't taken any medicine since then, either."

"Um…things change with time. At least see a physician before something absolutely terrible happens. I'm worried."

The doorbell rang.

She shook her head. "Have a ball explaining why you slept on the neighbor's lawn."

"You shouldn't have called the cops." He adjusted his housecoat and went to the door.

Parrish was amazed at the UPS man's size. He stood eight inches over Parrish, maybe nine. His blond hair balanced on his head as if it were a foreign object. His fingers reminded Parrish of jumbo Oscar Mayer franks; his knuckles of lug nuts.

"Good morning," Parrish said as a police car parked in the driveway.

"I'm looking for Parrish Clovis. I have a package for him."

Two uniformed officers stepped out of the car.

"How can I help you?"

Ace thrust the package into Parrish's arms. "You must sign for it."

The uniforms started up the driveway.

"What is it?" Parrish eyed the package. The cops lurching up the walk were in his peripherals, and he was rehearsing the lie he would tell.

"I do not know. I only deliver." Ace gave him an electronic pen and a digital Toshiba tablet.

A Hispanic officer nodded at Ace in passing and then faced Parrish. "We got a call about a missing person."

Ace headed for the truck and emailed Parrish's signature to his personal computer.

Parrish tore the package open. It was empty.

Everything beyond the handcrafted doors facing me, taunting me, was what I once loved. A love that was patient, kind. Neither was it envious nor boastful—just love. I stored no records of wrong, not until she had taken her mask off and showed me her ugly face.

Now, everything beyond the threshold of those doors, beyond the security system, is everything I hate worse than my mother.

Lightning parted the night again; thunder barked behind it. Call me crazy, but it seemed as if the thunder were cussing me like I were a little boy in need of scolding.

My BlackBerry glowed; its ring tone crooned a neo-soul tune by Vivian somebody. The sultry lyrics reminded me of what I must do: *Gotta go, gotta leave.* I wished I could blend with the rain and trickle down the sewer. I pressed SEND but didn't bother to say anything. I wasn't in a talkative mood. I gave the caller nothing more than a deep breath.

"Parrish, is you…everything okay?" Sade said.

Stupid question. What can be said about any man wanting to kill his wife and her lover? "I'm fine."

"Twenty minutes is left before you hafta cross the Holland Tunnel and come to the airstrip. Then, we home free."

Her raggedy cadence set fire to my loins' erogenous zones. It's strange how humans desire sex in the presence of death. Even sitting here staring at those doors I could smell Sade. Her pussy perfumed my mustache.

She said, "You there?"

Chapter 2

Murder. I had gotten away with it once; tonight was the perfect time to try my luck again.

The sky was dark and quarrelsome, reflective of my mood. Lightning split the night in two. The heavens cried a steady downpour of tears. The heavens' choice of pain purging was tears. Mine? Double homicide.

The sway of my windshield blades was hypnotizing, sedative even. They seemed to wipe the blur away from my vision. They seemed to wipe her ugliness away from my thoughts. The SUV's idling engine was smooth. Meditative. Healing.

Only a moment slipped by before *her* ugliness tormented me again.

My palms were slick with evidence of my nervousness. I gripped the steering wheel, thinking. I forced a fidgety foot to keep pressure on the brake. My worn-out brown eyes were fixated on the Italianate structure eleven yards ahead of me, a place that I was once proud to call home. Neighbors, passersby, and associates from our inner circle of influence considered this type of home a symbol of status, success. I, on the other hand, know that it represented four wasted years, failure, regret.

"Wish I were there with you."

"Is you sure you okay? Boy, you don't sound like it."

I put my eyes on the glove compartment. "I will be after tonight." My palms were still sweaty. My foot was still on the brake. The doors of that home were still taunting me. The rain was still pelting the windshield.

"Where are you?" She sounded irritated. "We gotta schedule to keep."

"Outside of my house...thinking."

"You done, then, ain't you?"

"No."

"No?"

"*No!*"

"Damn, boy, you 'bout to blow everything. You trippin'." Her voice was two octaves too damn high. "Hana deserves this. We done come this far; now ain't the time to be fuckin' thinking." She sighed in my ear, much louder than necessary—her ridiculous signature.

I hate it when she does that. I've hit myself upside the head several times for becoming involved with someone so...ghetto. I'd like to know what the hell I was thinking.

"You was s'posed to be done and on your way back to me. This plane gots to be in the sky before our cover is blown."

"Don't press me. I'm not in the mood. We'll make it."

"You scared. It ain't even difficult. Fuck that bitch."

I stared at the doors, thinking of all that I had been through.

She said, "Stay right there. I'm on my way. I ain't scared. I'll do it my damn self."

"I said, I'll take care of it."

A car horn was blown.

I studied the rearview; it studied me back, reflecting the pain trapped behind my eyes. There was a BMW with a missing headlight behind me. Behind it, from my Hoboken, New Jersey avenue, I could see the whore of America—the Statue of Liberty. Her crown and torch punctuated the night. I eased my fidgety foot from the brake.

Hoboken was a Hudson River city whose community was a cultural melting pot. The city had been long seasoned with writers, artists, singers, actors, professional athletes, and others. Most of us had chosen Hoboken because it was situated directly across the river from Manhattan. The commute to New York was swift and convenient.

The swift part would come in handy tonight.

It had never dawned on me that I was blocking the avenue this entire time.

I shut my headlights off and parked behind Hana's Mercedes. "Listen to me, Sade."

"Ain't I here?"

"I never want to feel this type of pain again. Every woman who's been in my life has hurt me. Promise me that it ends with you. I don't want to hurt anymore. I love—" My confession was interrupted by the roar of thunder.

"Boy, ain't I already done made that promise? How many times you wanna hear it? Keepin' it real, if I wasn't serious 'bout us, I wouldn't be mixed up in this bullshit with you. I woulda never aborted my baby for you." There was a pause that felt empty. "Love is a verb. Now is a damn good time to show me." She hung up.

Those ugly, ugly days rushed back. They poked their devious fingers at me. My eyes narrowed to slits. I opened the glove compartment and saw a Sig Sauer .9mm smiling at me.

Chapter 3

Pops had always warned me to be very careful when choosing a woman to love, because there was no telling who she'd be tomorrow. He only said that, or something similar, when the topic of my mother would unstitch our shaky peace, leaving us nauseous, causing my schizophrenia to spike, causing my sister to progress in her emotional dysfunction.

Pops' suggestion was that my sister and I approach love "like a hot bath. Try to ease a foot into it," he would say in his raspy baritone. "If it's too damn hot, change the water." One day I had invited Erienne home after school to work on a photography assignment. Pops took one look at us and said, "Don't ever change the water."

I wish that I had listened to Pops about Erienne, though.

So, what drives a motion-picture mogul to literally act out a role written for the Big Screen? How does love and its beauty transform to hate within the flicker of an eye? Listen closely because the answers are so embarrassing, I'll never tell this story to another soul.

The ruining of my existence, as far as I know, began four days after Hurricane Katrina had devastated Louisiana. Hana and I were stuck in traffic. We had been idling inside the Holland Tunnel for over an hour. An accident had shut down traffic in both directions. We had just left Manhattan's Theater District. It was our second viewing of Eric Myrieckes' stage play of *Fed Up Black Men*.

I could never get comfortable with the contemptuous looks I'm given when Hana and I are together in public. Let's face it: Black women hate to see a powerful black man with a woman whose roots don't begin in Africa, whose hair is straight without the help of a relaxer. Hana is an ethnic mutt, a Hungarian gypsy, so black women often felt that I didn't have any damn business bringing one of *them* to *our* social functions.

If it would put a smile on her face, I'd sit my black behind through a Klan rally dressed in Black Panther gear. Make no mistake about it, I loved my wife—dirty panties included.

She sighed and closed her eyes. "This is just great. Absolutely great." Being held hostage by our car had worn her patience transparent.

"We should be moving soon. The accident must really be bad." I glanced at her. "The play was good. I haven't laughed like that in a long time."

"Were you fond of the Spanish woman seated beside us tonight?" She never looked at me. She stayed focused on the ambulance and police lights ricocheting off of the tunnel's convex walls.

I remembered the exotic woman all too well. Each time her thigh had brushed against mine an electrical current shot through me. The animal in me could smell her pheromonal desire; there was no doubt in my mind that the pussy cat in her had smelled my sexual scent, too. I had imagined her measured purrs stimulated by my tongue each time we smiled at each other.

"Uhm, that was a question, of course. Did you like her?"

I tilted my hand in a seesaw motion. "She was so-so. What makes you ask?"

"Watched you watching her. You pretty much saw more of her than you did of the show. Would you have liked to invite her home with us?"

I thought for a moment, purposely. I didn't want to seem too eager, but I was praying to God that she had decided to entertain my fantasy. "With your consent, yes."

"Don't try it, Parrish." She glanced at me for the first time.

We traded a look.

I watched her painted lips part and her pink tongue sway as she spoke.

"The only way another woman...forget about it." She banged her head against the headrest twice. "Stupid, stupid traffic. This isn't happening."

Forget nothing. "Say it."

"I don't like repeating myself; it irritates me. You heard me say to forget it."

"Don't start, Han. I'm not in the mood to fight. You brought it up. I respected your position on the matter before we were married; respect it now."

Hana had a beautiful sandy-beach complexion. It covered her svelte body as if it were melted on. Her silky black hair ebbed down her back. She wore natural black pearls, matching earrings, and a matching bracelet. I could smell her apricot hair conditioner. It fascinated me to see her in evening gowns. They fit her curvy body like she had been poured into them.

Tonight her gown highlighted her breasts and emphasized her ass with an exclamation point. And the peek-a-boo split...the split traveling her defined thigh—courtesy of squats, extreme handball, and Hatha yoga—promised to guide me to her wet spot. Utopia.

The first time I had laid eyes on Hana, she was in my studio reading the script for the movie *The Grandfather Crime*. I had been transfixed by her potent femininity ever since. Even the way she batted her lashes made me stutter.

Rubbing her arms, she said, "It feels like a meat locker in here." She considered me for a moment. "Why do people in committed relationships cheat?"

I turned the AC down, stalling. She had thrown me with that one. I knew that the actress in her had steered the dramatic tone of that question. I think. Sometimes I couldn't tell when she was acting or just being Hana, which was a class act in itself. "Infidelity is rampant for a number of reasons, I suppose."

"The primary reason people cheat is because of their sexual differences," she said. "Sometimes people's needs change but they don't speak up. Zipping your lips, or saying no, in the bedroom is to birth a cheater." Her accent was stunning.

"In addition, money problems are worth mentioning. Read about it somewhere."

"It's actually only a matter of time before you cheat, if you haven't already. Not in the absence of love, but to simply gratify your sexual desires that I deny you at home."

"Say...say, for example, someone wanted to explore or live out a particular sexual act really badly, and their mate refuses, hinders them from the experience they seek, eventually they'll step outside the boundaries of their bedroom to quench the thirst."

"The boundaries of the bedroom." She gave me my words back and wet her lips. "Have you tipped outside of ours?"

"Bite your tongue, Han, and avoid a fight. I let you slide with calling me a cheat a minute ago." Now I wished they would clear the accident so we could be on our way.

She shifted her eyes toward me. Nothing else moved. "How long before you do cheat?" Only her eyes blinked. "How long before you leave our bedroom for that drink?"

I couldn't believe I had bitten the hook. "I don't know about you, but I'm married in the traditional sense. Your position isn't a surprise. It was understood before we were married. I made a conscious decision to circumcise my fantasies then. I'm not having second thoughts about my decision." A flicker of time passed as I gazed at the bumper-to-bumper traffic jam ahead of us. "Furthermore, since you seem to be operating in selective-hearing mode, I'll say it slower this time: a person who craves a sexual experience really badly, *for example*. I'm not that person. I'm down with a threesome wherever, whenever you're ready, if ever. But I'm not reinforcing my every thought with that reality; neither am I suppressing the idea."

"Did you imagine yourself having sex with that Spanish woman?"

"Han, where—"

"Did you screw her in your thoughts, Parrish?" Her words were deliberate.

I had thought about Spanish Fly and me forming a 69. Her full lips pulling my manhood into her scorching mouth, my tongue touring the seven wonders of her pussy. "Yeah, I pictured us making love to her. Where are we going with this conversation? Don't think you're going to ruin this evening with an argument. I'm getting some tonight, even if I have to take it."

"Of course you would, wouldn't you?" Her penciled brow rose.

"I won't be wacking off."

She frowned, thinking. "Don't offer me up that *making love* garbage; it would be nothing more than cheap sex. And you're lying; you only said *us* because you feel guilty about mentally cheating. Don't make me your accomplice." She was full-blown pissed.

I said, "Point is…"

"There is a point to all conversations." Her voice instantly changed to calm and soft, sending me mixed signals. "You have to be educated in the art of listening to get the point. Can I ask you a question?"

I exercised my right to remain silent, knowing that she'd interrogate anyway.

She considered me for several heartbeats. "If I were to tell you my secret fantasy, would you look at me different?" She fiddled with the diamond ring on her commitment finger.

That spiked my pulse. The last time she had done that she was having doubts about getting married. "I was under the impression that we entered this marriage with no secrets. You swore that you had no fantasies." I couldn't help but to think of what else my wife may have concealed.

"There is one. I was afraid to tell you." She lowered her head in shame. "I was afraid that you would consider me a slut and look at me through a stranger's eyes."

Chapter 4

Tonight, the Bar None rumble went down in an abandoned auto-body shop. A members-only crowd roared when Ace slammed Soul Snatcher, the people's champ, on the oily concrete.

This was child's play for Ace. He had mastered the Krav Maga style of hand-to-hand combat in the military; he was enjoying himself while performing it. To Ace, fighting was his sex, the only pleasure he knew.

Soul Snatcher was broken. He had never faced an opponent who grinned the entire fight. He had never felt like he was being knocked around by a John Deere backhoe, either. The applause was thunderous and boastful, but to Soul Snatcher it was tiny and distant.

Ace clenched his paw on top of Soul Snatcher's head and jerked him to his feet, effortlessly. "Next time I will ram you to Satan's basement," he said, his words slow. He wrecked his sloped forehead into Soul Snatcher's face, crunching it, forcing his battered body into the crowd.

The crowd shoved Soul Snatcher back into the battle square. Soul Snatcher fired a desperate punch and missed. Ace's mouth split into a smile. He grabbed Soul Snatcher from behind, slipped him into a guillotine choke, and stood erect.

"Might as well pay up now, buddy," an Amerasian man said to a squat white man standing beside him. "When he puts that move on 'em, it's over."

Soul Snatcher felt like a boa constrictor was wrapped around his neck. His feet splayed six inches above the concrete.

Ace walked to each end of the battle square, taunting the crowd with their chump. He whispered to Soul Snatcher, "It is time." He squeezed, using only a fraction of his *real* strength. He hadn't done that since the fight had begun.

Soul Snatcher's neck cracked.

The room screeched to a halt when the dull sound registered. Soul Snatcher fell in a dead heap. Ace came on himself.

✪✪✪

The quiet between us was so still I could hear the wheels turning in her head. "Loving you is a way of life. It's my religion. I can only see you with one set of eyes."

She lifted her head and showed me her even teeth. "People voice things every day with good intentions, but tomorrow's reality is entirely different."

"Han, stop acting. Tell me about this fantasy. If you're the only one who knows about it, it'll always be a fantasy."

She canted her head and laughed. A nervous laugh.

"In a relationship, you must *be* what you want to have."

Uh-oh, she went Sufi mystic.

"If you prefer to experience unconditional love," she said, "you have to be unconditional. You must be prepared to give exactly what you want for yourself."

"Okay, Yoda, where is this going? As a matter of fact, this conversation is over. Jesus, would they clear this traffic?" I started imagining Bin Laden and his buddies blowing the tunnel. I turned the radio on to clear my thoughts.

The personality was giving listeners information on where they should send donations to Hurricane Katrina victims. I wrote the address down and caught a glimpse of myself in the rearview. My paper bag complexion amplified a set of brown eyes that had witnessed too much, but wanted to see so much more.

She thumbed the radio off. "You promised to give me anything and everything I ever wanted."

"And I meant it."

"Anything?"

"I pride myself on being a man of my word."

She lifted her lashes and examined me from the corner of an eye. "It is a fact that all women want to be whores for their men, whether they literally act out the impulse or fantasize about it in their thoughts. The same way you screwed that Spanish woman tonight."

My forehead wrinkled. "Okay. That was enlightening."

"I'll... " She hesitated. "I'll give you your fantasy if you'll fulfill mine."

In my mind I was jumping up and down shouting, *Booyah!* But on the outside, I played it cool. "I don't have any idea what your fantasy is. Never knew it existed until ten minutes ago."

"Let me be your whore for one night." She blinked. Nothing else moved. "One night."

For a few heartbeats I was stunned. I felt warm in all the right places.

All of a sudden, I had no idea of who this woman was. "Ah...okay. What do you want to do? Dress up? Do it in some wild place? Role play? What?"

"You're so self-centered it makes me ill." She pushed her palms across her breasts, down the gown, along her thighs. She held my gaze and wet her lips. She retraced her path, hiking the gown past her hips. She was panti-less. Her pussy was bald. I had been trying to get her to shave for me for years, but she refused to cut it all.

"You have to be willing to offer what you desire." She licked her longest finger and then buried it inside her pussy.

I almost choked. "What did you do with my wife?" I was having trouble applying meaning to this. This was out of character for a woman with whom I have to fill out a request form to screw doggy style.

She clamped her eyes, bit her lip, and pressed her head against the seat. "You enjoy this, correct?" Her finger disappeared again and again and again.

"Yeah, but..." I scratched my head. "Is this Step Two from an improve-your-sex-life article?" I wasn't sure whether to enjoy the sudden change or to take her to an exorcist.

While strumming her clitoris, she began to wail like she had never before. She shifted, facing me. Her back on the door. Her foot on my shoulder. My mouth watered when I saw her creamy skin and pink insides. A beautiful contrast. I could hear the wetness sing to me as she played her instrument.

"Allow me to be your whore for a night. Say yes, Parrish. I'll share our bed with another woman."

Her sex-induced aroma invaded my sense of smell. "You can be my whore." My manhood was all grown up and aching.

"Would you enjoy watching me finger myself more often?"

I couldn't speak. I just nodded.

Chapter 5

The man stood several inches taller than the six-foot perch that the African parrot sat on. He looked down on the gray creature. "Dumb bird. I bet you just eat and shit, don't you?" He tried to touch it. "Can you talk?"

The parrot pinched his finger and drew blood. That was a warning.

"Ow! You rotten motherfucker. Do that shit again." He sucked his finger.

He took his cell phone out and used the speed dial feature.

The phone rang twice.

The parrot watched.

"Yeah," a husky voice on the other end of the phone answered.

"It's started."

"Good."

"Won't be long now." He frowned at the bird.

"Awwk, suck my dick," the parrot said, flapping its wings as if it were throwing punches.

❂❂❂

She gasped when she pushed her finger in again. "You're not understanding what I'm saying, Parrish. I truly want to be your whore." She was deep within herself. Her leg began to tremble.

I licked the sole of her foot. "Make me understand."

"Take-your meat out. I want to blow it." Her breathing had elevated.

"Are you on drugs?" Either I was dreaming or she was under the influence. "It's bumper-to-bumper traffic. The last thing we need to do is get caught out here like two horny teenagers. That will be devastating to our careers. We don't need that type of media coverage."

"To hell with the tabloids. Let me suck your dick!"

I didn't even know she knew that word.

She unzipped my slacks. "Don't be such a wimp."

I couldn't believe it. I was nervous and the flashing police lights scared the hell out of me. But her mouth felt so good I had tears in my eyes. "I promise...you can be my whore any time you want. Umm," I moaned. "I won't look at you different." I ran my fingers through her hair while she showed me how much she loved me.

"This is being an adventurous slut. Don't muddle this with being your whore." She ran her tongue along my manhood, leaving a damp path, then kissed the bull's-eye. "You care to know what I'm imagining right now?" Her eyes sustained pure lust. "My fantasy, Parrish?"

"Tell me. Please tell me." I guided her head back into my lap. Nervousness had abandoned me. *To hell with the tabloids.* "Tell me, and I'll make it happen, Han."

"I want you to screw me hard while I suck another man's meat."

"What!" I shriveled like a newborn and pushed her off of me in one heartbeat. Instantly pissed.

She fixed me with an evil look that I had never witnessed before. "You were born with one dick, Parrish."

Even the tone of her voice was different; her accent made me sick to my stomach.

"I actually have three holes, two of which need to be filled at the same time. I crave it. You're clueless to the number of dicks I've sucked in my mind while you were screwing me." She considered me, eyes as serious as death. "I'm worn out with pretending. I desire the experience."

Maybe it was the fact that my fragile ego had been crushed, but for the first time in my thirty-one years on this earth, I could empathize with why men hit women. My initial impulse was to reach over and slap the soul from her body. I couldn't believe she had the audacity to tell me she was mentally with other men while we were making love. I had *thought* I was putting in work humping her like a jackrabbit. Who had all that clawing and panting been for, me or them? "Han, what is wrong with you?" I had a few more thoughts. "Oh, I get it." I punched the car horn. "This whole conversation and your strange behavior were contrived from the start."

"No, *I* get it. What's good enough for *you*, isn't good enough for me." She folded her arms beneath her breasts, sullen and angry. "You want me to welcome another woman into our bedroom. Not to mention...she and I are to fondle. My fantasy doesn't require you and another man to screw one another. I only desire that you and another man screw me."

"Don't-say-that-again." My breath caught. "If you do, I'll knock your whole head off. You've made your point. I'll never suggest a threesome again."

"This wasn't an effort to wound you or discredit your lovemaking. Of course, I'm serious. I want it. God, I want it."

"Shut the fuck up!" It was official. I was mad as a mother. From time to time I use foul language in my head. When it's verbalized, I am usually beyond pissed. A cold chill ran through me. I have never hit a woman in my life, but I was now on the verge.

She said, "People cheat because of their sexual differences. It's only a matter of time before we both seek our desires outside of our bedroom." She faced me; a complete stranger. "I'm too adult to sneak around. I won't. Let's get it out of our systems. You get her; I get him. Whores for one night. It suits you to watch two men give it to a woman on your porno tapes."

I hit her with all of my might. Her lip split. I banged her head against the window, trying to knock her foul thoughts out. I punched and punched and punched. I even bit her as hard as I could. Well, that's what I imagined myself doing. I puffed up my jaws and then let the air go slow. "Hana. Hana, please don't say it again. If you do, I'll break my father's—may he rest in peace—number one rule and kick your entire ass."

Chapter 6

Hana Kaffka fired a handball against the wall of their indoor court. The faster it recoiled, the harder she struck it. She refused to miss. A miss meant failure. Game over. She had been abusing the handball for forty-one minutes straight. Sweat soaked her outfit and slicked the floor beneath her. She loved to hear the ball scream when it wrecked into the wall. It was stress-relieving. The intensity of the stress Hana Kaffka was about to endure, a screaming handball wouldn't help. No, sir.

✪✪✪

Two hours later I had fed Rudy, my mean-spirited bird, showered, and was now lying in bed staring at the ceiling. I stared at the ceiling's stucco pattern so long, without blinking, that my eyes burned. It was driving me crazy to know that I had been sleeping beside a complete stranger. I couldn't believe that she'd fixed her mouth to ask me to share her with another man. I didn't appreciate that image, and I couldn't get the picture out of my head. She was right about one thing, though:

what's good enough for me, isn't good enough for her—not in *that* light.

Rudy flew into the room and landed on the nightstand.

The phone rang.

Rudy watched me.

I turned on my side and stared at Rudy and the phone. I assumed that Hana would answer. After the fourth ring, I told Rudy to move.

"Awwk, asshole."

"Same to you." I reached for the phone. Rudy's previous owners should be ashamed of themselves for teaching him just about every cuss word and cruddy phrase in the book.

"Dumb fuck."

I ignored Rudy. "Hello," Hana and I said at the same time.

Rudy flew away.

Tuesday said, "Hey, little brother," her words dragging.

I heard Hana click off. "What's going on with you?"

"Intoxicated and looking for some action; at least two hours and eight inches of it."

"Figures."

"Something must've crawled up your ass and got stuck. From the sound of it, you need a drink, some dope, and some sex, too."

"Get yourself together, and then call me back. There are some things on my mind; it's just not a good time for me." I wasn't in the mood for my sister's nonsense. "Say goodbye. I'm hanging up."

"Don't." I could hear her fumble something. When the rustling stopped, she said, "I need to say thank you."

"For what?" I closed my eyes as if it would erase the image of Hana sucking—

"Having my back. It's no secret that I'm not that bright, and I tend to destroy almost everything. If I didn't have you to run things, I'd ruin everything Daddy left us."

"You're drunk," I said, watching Rudy parade across the wet bar. "Where are you?"

"In Beverly Hills, at Mr. Chow's."

"Go to your condo and get some rest. Call me back in the morning. I want to talk to you about a company merger."

"Mergers, board meeting, films, and actors are not my thing. I don't need to be a part of those discussions. Right now I'm high. I'm zooming pretty fast, and I'm having an emotional outburst. So, shut the hell up and listen, would you?" There was a pause. "I wish you were older and had inherited the majority of Upscale Pictures." She made a divergence from the *emotional outburst* to order drinks.

I heard her tell the waiter that she wanted two martinis. "Who's with you?"

"Me, myself, and...uhm...let me check. Me."

"If you keep drinking and driving, abusing your body with drugs, and having irresponsible sex, I will inherit Upscale and all your wealth. You'll be dead or wish you were." I thought about our mother.

"You act like I'm a crack Martian or something. Everything I do is recreational, even sex. You know how I feel about men, plus I can't honor a commitment to myself. Don't expect me to change. I like to get high and have sex while I'm high."

There was a suffocating silence.

"I miss Daddy so much, Parrish."

While my pops was on his deathbed, he made me promise to take care of Tuesday. He left the majority of Upscale's shares to her, hoping it put her on the straight and narrow. He thought that giving her the responsibility of carrying on his legacy would compel her to clean up her act. I knew what my pops had really instructed me to do: don't allow Tuesday to kill herself or to destroy Upscale. I wouldn't let him down. I was hoping that an active role in the company would change her ways, too. So far, she hadn't changed a bit; she had only passed her responsibility on to me.

I told her, "I miss Daddy, too."

"DMX just came in. Think that Karrine Stephens chick had him barking; before the night is over, I'll have him fetching and playing dead. I'll call you back."

"I thought we were having a moment."

"I'm gonna see if he'll smoke a joint with me. Gotta go." She hung up.

I held the phone until it started screaming at me.

Rudy said, "Awwk, asshole."

I wondered why I even fed him.

The elevator doors eased open on the far side of the bedroom.

"Stinkin' slut." Rudy had that right.

Hana stood there. She wore a low-cut tan camisole, a matching thong, and a pair of heels. She had wine glasses and a bottle of Monticello Sangiovese. That was a rare choice. She had to pull that one from the wine cellar.

"Make up with me...please."

"There's an image in my head that I'm not appreciative—"

"Don't talk, Parrish; just fuck me."

This had to be a clone of my wife. Hana would never use the F word.

She went to the wet bar and poured drinks.

Rudy flew back to my nightstand.

"Anything that doesn't suit you, deal with the issue in bed. I'll be more cooperative," she said.

Her camisole was so short that I had a perfect view of her ass. I indulged myself in every movement it presented. She threw back a drink, refilled it, and turned to me. The expression on her face was different, intense.

"Awwk, don't trust the bitch," Rudy said.

Sometimes I wondered if he knew what he was talking about.

"I'm going to glue your beak shut," Hana said. "You're the devil."

I could hear our neighbor's irritating dog yapping in the distance. I probably hated that dog more than Hana hated Rudy.

She handed me a drink and told me I would need it because of what I was about to experience. I thanked her and watched this strange woman peel the camisole off her body.

She downed her second drink and then let the empty glass fall to the carpet. "Goodness gracious, there's a fire blazing deep inside me that hungers for extinguishing."

I set my empty glass beside Rudy. He looked at me as if I had a booger hanging from my nose.

I ignored him.

Why shouldn't I play along? This may never happen again. "Where's the fire, ma'am?"

"In here, Mr. Fireman. Right here." Her hand disappeared inside of the thong; her nipples tightened.

"A fire in a place like that can get out of hand if it's not taken care of. To get that nasty thing under control, the first thing I'll need to do is get past these." I hooked her thong with my index finger.

She squirmed at the bedside as she wiggled the thong down her legs. "That should accommodate."

She yanked the sheet back. Protruding through the vent of my boxers was evidence of my interest in the wildfire burning within her. She took my interest in her hand and then massaged it a few moments before straddling it and guiding it into the wet heat. The sound she made when receiving me was erotic, addictive.

"Put my fire out. It's so hot for you, Mr. Fireman." She kissed me while bouncing on my interest.

Our tongues danced to the rhythm of our winding bodies. She sat upright, arched her back, and began to joyride. She made love to me with the same passion and aggression with which she played handball. This was better than our wedding night.

I closed my eyes, loving the energy surrounding the moment. I felt sluggish, heavy with passion. The neighbor's yapping dog didn't even bother me anymore. Behind the lids of my eyes there was darkness. A blackness I had never witnessed. The thought of our conversation in the car hit me. I opened my eyes to see Hana gobbling a huge black man's manhood. My anger returned.

"Awwk, stinkin' slut," I heard Rudy say.

This time I squeezed my eyes as tight as I could. That image had to go. The next time I lifted my exhausted lids, there were several angry cops standing over me.

Chapter 7

I looked into the faces of four city cops.

"Rich bastards, think you're above the law. You get a fucking thrill out of beating on innocent women." It was the white cop who jabbed me with a nightstick. "Turn over; hands behind your back. I'm dying for you to make me ask again."

For some reason I felt like I had been sucker-punched. It pained me to move my jaw. After a few seconds, I squinted and said, "What?" My response time was malfunctioning. My brain was struggling to log on. I felt strange, and I had the chills. There was a dark haze lingering above me. I had a headache that seemed as if it would literally split my head into tiny pieces. I blinked the cloudiness away, and then my ears uploaded.

Hana was crying somewhere in my immediate surroundings.

"Hana!" I sat bolt upright and noticed blood on our linen.

"Goddamnit, it bit me," someone said, and then I heard Rudy's wings flapping.

Two black cops pounced on me, forcing me to my

stomach while the white cop, who looked as if he wanted to murder me, handcuffed me.

"She won't be your punching bag again, buddy," the white cop said, pressing a narrow knee in my back. "Mr. Parrish Clovis, you're under arrest for rape and assault." He went on to advise me of my rights. The right to this, the right to that.

I refused. There was no way I could keep my mouth shut. Were they retarded? I had to let them know: "I don't know what the hell is going on."

"Awwk, bullshit," Rudy said.

They dragged me from my bed and wrapped a sheet around my nakedness. Hana was sitting on a wicker chair talking to another cop, her back to me.

"Hana, what is the meaning of this? Why are all of these...these cops here?"

She stood and faced me.

My knees buckled.

A squat Salvadorean woman and a thin white man came into the room. Both paramedics rushed to aid Hana.

I trembled as I studied Hana's gruesome sight. Blood stained her camisole. Her lip was busted up pretty bad. The left side of her face was swollen. If I didn't know my wife from the neck down, I wouldn't have recognized her. Her right eye was closed involuntarily, a nasty bruise coloring it. There were black and blue marks scattered about her neck and arms. She looked as if she had gone ten rounds with the heavyweight champion of the world.

"Aw, baby, who did this to you?" I tried to go to her.

To comfort her. To hold her. To tell her that I would fix everything. Those were fruitless notions; the cops made sure of it.

"I hate you, Parrish. You're absolutely insane. How could you do this to my face? It suits you to see me not revive my acting career. I can't get a role looking like this." Tears fell from her good eye. "It only took one time for you to hurt me. I promise you'll be prosecuted in the worst way."

I started having respiratory complications when she accused me of hurting her in such a foul way. "Why...I wouldn't do—"

"The nerve of this guy," a square-chinned cop near Hana said. "Get this asshole outta here." He shooed me as if I were some type of undesirable. "This prick has put Mrs. Kaffka through enough."

The Salvadorean medical technician kneeled in front of Hana. "We're gonna need you to come to the hospital for a rape test due to the nature of..." She glanced over her shoulder at me, and then shifted back to Hana. "You understand."

"Tell them I wouldn't do this. Go ahead, tell them, Han."

"Awwk, goddamn liar," Rudy said, walking the counter-top of the wet bar.

"Shut up, Rudy."

"Fuck you." He flapped his wings.

The cops looked at Rudy and then ushered me into the hall.

"Hana, please tell them." I continued to plead to her as they forced me down the stairs. I heard Rudy call me a goddamn liar again. A minute later, I found myself in the backseat of an idling police cruiser.

I read the white cop's nameplate, *Duval Michaels*, when he poked his head into the car.

He said, "There must be a God. Had I been the first to respond, I'd have put a bullet in your head. You niggers—rich or not—don't have business screwing around with our women. You'd think that Emmett Till nigger would've been lesson enough. You bastards like to fuck and abuse our women but aren't man enough to admit it. I guess you think you're indirectly paying us back for slavery. At least we owned up to raping and lynching your people. Fucking coward." He slammed the door. "I'm glad this is my last night as a uniformed officer," he said, walking away.

I wondered if he'd still feel that way if he knew that Hana wasn't White. The neighbor's irritating Rottweiler was standing at the fence yapping. I closed my eyes and thought. Had I hurt Hana? I remembered the anger, the sex, the anger, and then everything went blank. I peeped at our bedroom's bay window.

She was standing there.

When our eyes found one another, she shut the drapes. I would have never guessed that when I climbed into bed a few hours ago, my face would be on the front page of every newspaper in the country by morning.

Chapter 8

Tuesday awoke in a rank pool of vomit. Her hair was matted with chunks of decomposing broccoli and asparagus. Each time the phone rang, the buzz rattled her brain. She propped herself on an elbow and tried to catch up with the spinning kitchen.

The phone rang again.

"Dammit, I'm coming," she said, smearing the vomit on her mouth with her shirttail. She saw a half-burnt joint on the marble floor in the spotlight of the open refrigerator. She reached for it.

And the phone rang.

She pulled her purse from the table and dumped its contents on the floor, in search of a lighter.

She lay her back against the marble, blinking the ceiling fan in and out of focus. She inhaled a cloud of marijuana and cocaine smoke, hoping it would get rid of the jitters.

And...the phone rang.

She crawled to it and yanked the handset from the wall by its cord. "What?"

"Don't ask me because I don't have any answers," Parrish said. "Come get me. I'm in jail."

"Not now, please."

"I'm serious. Upscale's jet is already at the office in Malibu. You're the only one who can help me."

"Aw, Parrish, Hana's closer," Tuesday said around the smoldering joint. "Have her come for you. It's four in the morning here."

"I'm asking you. And could you bring me some clothes?"

"You're really serious, aren't you?"

He didn't answer.

She sighed. "Fuck! I'll be there." She hung up and drew hard on the joint. "This drug shit is killing me." She thought about how much she hated Catherine.

❋❋❋

It wasn't until 11:00 that morning when I made bail. Tuesday was outside of the precinct, leaning against our limo, smoking a Newport. She might not be on crack, but she was definitely a functional junkie. She had lost at least ten pounds since last month. The whites of her eyes were stained yellow; her sockets were dark. Her cheeks were sunk in, and she kept wiping the button of her nose with a ball of tissue. Her clothes seemed to have no defining purpose; they just hung there as if she were a hanger. The partying and the mileage she had been putting her body through were beginning to fade her beauty to zero.

"Well, oh *fucking* well," she said, "the perfect brother ain't so perfect after all. I don't feel like that big of a fuck-up anymore. I never thought I'd live to see this day." She handed me the *Home News Tribune*. "This is a goddamn change."

"I haven't done anything."

"Don't lie to me. It's usually me getting picked up from the slammer after a mischievous night. This morning it's you. Ah, that means you did something."

I unfolded the paper and came down with a migraine.

MOTION-PICTURE MOGUL
SEXUALLY ASSAULTS
MOVIE-STAR SPOUSE

Beneath the bold headline was a picture of Hana and me, taken on the set of her last Oscar-nominated film.

"Let's get the hell away from here." Tuesday canted her head toward a group of TV reporters. "Can't do TV right now; I look like shit."

She had that right.

"It was a long night, teaching that old dog how to do new tricks."

The school of reporters clambered toward us like a pack of cockroaches after an abandoned plate of food. A flabby Korean woman led them. That was the first time I'd ever seen a fat Korean. She was followed by a lanky black man lugging a minicam on his shoulder.

"Give us something, Mr. Clovis." The flabby Korean shoved a microphone at me. "Why did you do it? Would you care to comment on reports of your unstable mental condition?" She took a deep breath. I lost mine. "Sources reveal that you've been battling mental health issues since childhood."

"Are you implying that I'm some type of fruit loop? You people are the crazy ones."

Tuesday tugged on my arm. "Get in the car. Jeanette said not to answer any of these assholes' questions without talking to her."

The tallest of the six reporters scowled at Tuesday and then turned to me. "According to a candid interview given to us this morning by Mrs. Hana Kaffka, you've been secretly seeing a psychologist. What is your diagnosis?"

Tuesday opened the car door. "Get in."

I was stunned. I couldn't believe Hana would tell them that.

Another thirty-something reporter said, "We're having some discrepancies about the medication you're prescribed. Care to clear it up?"

Tuesday pulled. "Come on."

The flabby Korean fired another question: "The violent display of aggression toward your wife; did that outburst result from your mental health? And, Mr. Clovis, do you plan on taking an insanity plea when this case goes to court?"

I broke away from Tuesday's grip. "I'm not on medication! I do not have violent goddamn behavior." I snatched the microphone from the Korean and slammed it to pieces. "I am a perfectly sane man." I grabbed her by her shirt and yanked her to her tiptoes. "Do I act like I have a goddamn mental problem, lady?"

Someone else pushed a TV camera inches away from my face. "Yes, you do seem to have a problem, Mr. Clovis. It's also obvious how easy it was for you to assault Mrs. Kaffka. But tell us what pushed you to the point where you felt it was necessary to rape your wife? Her fans would like to know."

"Dammit, Parrish, get in the fucking car."

Chapter 9

Parrish steadied himself on his knees to peer through the keyhole. *"Your thirteenth birthday is too far away. We can't stay here, not that long."* He wiped blood away from his eyes. He was irritated by the mess smeared across his behind.

"I'm only doing this for you," Tuesday said, stepping out of her underwear. *"No matter what I have to do, I'm gonna—"*

"Get the hell away from that door," Catherine said, walking into the room. *"And get your naked ass over here."* She put a laced joint to Tuesday's lips. *"Hit this. It'll make you feel good; make everything feel better; take the soreness away."*

Tuesday choked on the smoke. *"You don't care."*

Catherine smacked Tuesday—hard. *"Don't be wastin' my shit. Hit it again and hold it in."*

She took the French braid out of Tuesday's hair. Her ringlets fell past her shoulders. Catherine sprayed her with perfume and then covered her lips with red lipstick. *"Sex is nothing. It means nothing, you hear me? No emotions or feelings are attached to it. If sex isn't for your pleasure, it's used to get what you want. Understand?"*

Use it to get me and my brother away from you. *"Yes, Catherine."*

She cupped Tuesday's chin and spoke through clenched teeth, "I'm your mother, you disrespectful little bitch." She stormed out.

On the outside of the bedroom, Catherine examined the ten-dollar bag of heroin that Reverend Conrad Tharp had given her. She looked into his blue eyes. "Gimme some more and I'll let you have her till morning."

"Stop begging and unlock the door."

She let Reverend Conrad in and looked at Tuesday. "He pays good; treat him nice."

"Don't bother us." He pushed Catherine out and slammed the door. He turned to Tuesday, admired her nakedness, and unbuckled his pants.

She lay down on the mattress, staring at the closet. I'm only doing this for you, Parrish.

Parrish peered through the keyhole; Tuesday was buried beneath a sweaty white man. He could smell the stink of the mattress seeping under the closet door. It was more rank than the smell of his shitty ass.

Chapter 10

"You're an idiot," Tuesday said, chastising me as the limo eased away from the curb. "Those reporters will have tried and convicted you by the evening news." She shook her head twice.

I guess that meant she was double disgusted.

"Look, I've never been a Hana fan—not even as a person. I only put up with the gypsy bitch because you think you love her. But you didn't have any business putting your hands on her." She considered me. "You know how I feel about that shit. She's a woman. When it gets to the point you feel the need to hit, it's time to call it quits."

I said, "This isn't true," tossing the newspaper on her lap. "None of it." I opened and closed my mouth, working out the pain. It felt like someone had sucker-punched me.

"Stop lying." She put the point of a finger on the paper. "Lie to them, but don't you dare lie to me. I was with Hana this morning while she was being interviewed. I saw exactly what you did to her."

"I never hit her or any other woman. I love Hana. You

don't deliberately hurt the people you love. I need to see her and straighten all this out."

She hit me in the chest with the side of a fist. "She doesn't want to see you, pervert. You remind me so much of Catherine right now. I suppose you didn't force Hana to have sex, either? You even told her you would take it."

"I was joking. I didn't force myself on her." I rubbed my chest. "Keep your hands to yourself."

She hit me again—harder. "You're pathetic. Did you keep your hands to yourself when Hana begged you to stop?" Now she was on my side of the car hitting me.

I held her wrist and avoided her hurt eyes in order to gather my thoughts.

"Now you don't have nothing to say, fucking punk." She tugged herself free. "Say something. I hate what you did to her. You know how I feel about men taking advantage. But I'm your sister; I'm with you, right or wrong. So keep the lies out of our conversations. I hate it when you lie." She lit a joint. "You had to be drunk to act that way. Hana looks really bad. What happened last night?"

"You're the one who looks bad." I snatched the joint and threw it out of the window. "Look at you. If you're not a crackhead, you're not far from it. Your hair is a mess, your clothes are about to fall off, and you're starting to look like *your* mother." I couldn't stand to look at her anymore.

"Fuck you! Don't make this about me. I jumped out of bed and threw something on to come see about your ass." She sucked her teeth. "This is the thanks I get?" She dug a prescription bottle from her purse. "Were you ever gonna tell me about this?"

"About what?"

"Stop! Your medicine. Your shrink. Hana gave me these."

"Those are not mine. I haven't seen a therapist or taken medicine since high school; you know that."

"You just insist on lying. The proof is in my hand and you're gonna lie to my face." She began to read from the label: "Parrish Clovis, 1224 First Born Lane—"

"Let me see that." I took the bottle from her and read the remaining information: 150 Mg of Lithium Carbonate was prescribed on April 12 of 2005, *just about five months ago*, around the time I had awoken in my neighbor's yard in the nude. It was recommended that I take one capsule twice a day to stabilize my behavior. "Tuesday, I have no reason to lie. You have to believe me: I haven't seen these a day in my life."

"I watched Hana take them from your medicine cabinet."

I said it again real slow: "I haven't seen these a day in my life. Please believe me." I didn't know what any of this was suggesting, but I feared that it was starting again. Maybe it wasn't Hana who was acting strange. It may have been me all along.

"Believe you," Tuesday said with a smirk on her lips. "Hell, nah, I don't believe your lying ass. Every time the stakes are high, you lie." Her eyes narrowed and her jaw-bone throbbed. She was pissed. "That's your name and address on the bottle. Hana said you stopped taking your medicine and seeing your psychiatrist a month ago yesterday. Somebody beat the hell out of Hana last night, and it was only you and her there. You tell me why I should believe you?"

I considered her point of view long and hard. "I can't remember what happened. It's like I blacked out or something."

"Then it's possible you beat Hana's ass and raped her, just like the paper says, while you were in this *black area*, right?"

She had a point. I was reluctant to speak. I took the easy way out and answered with a shrug.

"Jeanette will know what to do." She held her hand out. "Give me fifty dollars."

I took my billfold out and calculated the money. "I'm not lying."

"Psst, yeah right. Convince the jury, because Hana is gonna prosecute."

I handed her the money. "What's that for?"

"The reefer you threw out the window."

✪✪✪

"Shh!" Jeanette Daniels, our lawyer, shushed me. "I'm concentrating." She relaxed her beefy shoulders and stole a few moments gazing down the driving range. She aimed the wedge at the golf ball, wiggled her wide hips a bit, and with a fluid hook swing, she whacked the ball.

Our eyes followed its flight past the 250-yard marker, the 300-yard marker, then bounce and lie near the screening that protected Interstate 95 motorists from hard hitters like Jeanette. She rolled a Cuban cigar around in her mouth, spat its juice, and plucked another ball from her $5.25 bucket. She was an attractive, early-fifties black woman. The gray hairs peppering her temples verified her wisdom. She always struck me as if she weren't comfortable with her gender.

She cracked another ball, sending it near the interstate on the fly, no bounce. She grinned with the cigar still in her mouth and then remembered I was there and glared at me. She gave me that same disgusted look that Tuesday had given me twenty minutes ago. "I heard everything you had to say." She pointed to one of several flat screens on the walls of the clubhouse. "I saw you show your ass on live television, too. Now let me put some clarity on this situation."

"I wish somebody would make sense of it." I plopped down on the lounging sofa facing the range. Its leather sighed under my weight. "I'm scared and confused, Jeanette. They're saying I hurt Hana. I don't even remember what happened last night."

She spat again. "Your doctor said your condition wouldn't allow you to be aware of last night's events, which can be a plus for my defense."

"Aren't you hearing me? I haven't been to a psychologist. I don't know a doctor named Lucinda Rodriguez."

Jeanette cracked another ball. "I spoke with her this

morning, Parrish. I know how embarrassing this must be. I'm also aware of the lengths you and Hana went to in order to keep this private, but I'm the one you need to talk to."

"You're making me second-guess myself and it's not a good feeling." I thought about everything that had happened up until the blur occurred. "It's like I'm a stranger in my own skin. I don't have any idea of what you're talking about."

This woman standing here with a cigar dangling from her mouth had known me since I was a nine-year-old boy. She had known Tuesday and me since we had escaped Cleveland and found our pops in Jersey. Now, twenty-two years later, she talked to me as if I had been dropped off on earth ten minutes ago. I stared at a caged tractor that was clearing the field of golf balls.

"This isn't looking good from a legal perspective at all." She gestured to a manila folder a few cushions down. "First things first. Your doctor—"

I frowned at her.

"I mean, Ms. Rodriguez. She would only give me limited information. You have to go to her office and sign a medical release. It's standard practice."

"There isn't any information to release." This was unbelievable. "You would think that I'd know if it were."

"That remains to be seen. Look at it this way: What do you have to lose? Prove there aren't any records. If you can't, get them to me. You're in a criminal and financial mess. If we can't work out a formal resolution between

Hana and yourself, those records may save your ass."

"I just need to talk to her." I shook my head in defeat, not understanding what life was throwing at me. "I'll straighten this out once I talk with her." I had a flashback of her blood-soaked camisole, the chatter from police radios, and the paramedics. I became sick to my stomach. I stuck my head in Jeanette's bucket of golf balls and emptied all that was inside me.

"Damn, that stinks. Cover it with something." She frowned. "Are you all right?"

Chapter 11

Tuesday kept an eye on Catherine and Reverend Conrad from the concealed shadows of the hallway. She wished that it were a dream, but what she was hearing was all too real—worse than a nightmare. She forced down the knot in her throat and prayed that Catherine wouldn't give in.

"I've been very patient," Reverend Conrad said. "I want the boy."

Catherine was sitting on what was left of the sofa, looking into his liquid blue eyes. "Take Tuesday; you like her."

"I like the idea of the boy more."

"But you've had Tuesday. I always make sure she smells pretty for you and wears the red lipstick you like. She's always taken care of you."

"Now my needs lie with Parrish. He's fresh."

Catherine removed the .32 automatic from her lap and slid it between two cushions.

"Come on, Conrad. I'm sick. I need something bad. Real bad. My bones are hurting." She scratched a pus-filled lesion on her arm.

"I have needs," his voice sour. "You promised him to me."

"But Tuesday—"

"*This is the best I'll do for the boy.*" *He showed her three dime-bags of heroin.*

Tuesday crossed her fingers. No, Catherine, don't do it.

Catherine's mouth watered. "*You can have me and Tuesday together. I swear we'll make it good to you.*"

"*To hell with you. You can't even get my dick hard.*" *He put the heroin in his pocket and went for the front door.*

"*What you doing, man?*"

"*Leaving.*"

Tuesday took a deep breath, relieved.

"*Okay, okay, gimme the dope.*" *She sat at the edge of the cushion with her hand out.* "*It's time he...he started earning his keep. Give it to me.*"

Tuesday took another deep breath. But this time she began to undress.

Catherine stuck her hand out farther. "*Come on, man, give it to me. This monkey is heavy on my back.*"

"*Take me to the boy and then you can do what you do.*"

"*Just give me one bag; I'll clean him up for you. You're gonna take pictures of him too, right? Come on, Conrad.*"

"*Take the dope, let me in the room with him, and don't bother me.*"

Tuesday strutted into the room naked, switching her hips, carrying a tube of lipstick. She laced her fingers with his. "*I been waiting for you. Would you help me put this on?*" *She offered him the lipstick.*

He stared at her bare mound and licked his lips.

Chapter 12

"No, I'm not okay," I said, staring at my vomit. I was sure that I would spill my guts again. I heard someone in the tee-box beside us smack a golf ball. "Everybody seems to have an idea about what's going on in my life but me." My jaw was still aching.

Jeanette helped me to my feet and gave me a hanky. "After last night, this shouldn't come as a surprise: Hana is filing for a divorce." She picked up the manila folder she had gestured to earlier as I settled back into my seat. "Parrish, how could you do something like this without consulting with me first?" She shook the folder at me. "I've been your family's attorney...it seems like forever. I watched your father single-handedly build everything you and Tuesday own today. Your father involved me in all of his legal affairs. I can't understand why you don't do the same." She thrust the folder at me. "You ruined yourself when you entered into a lopsided agreement like this."

I took the folder. "What are you talking about? All of my legal decisions are made with your advice."

"You sent me a package two weeks ago." The cigar bounced around. "Don't you even remember that?"

"I had Andrea send you the Docuversion merger proposal to look over last Friday, but I haven't sent you anything prior to that, or authorized anything to be sent to you on my behalf."

She squared her shoulders and cracked another ball. She shot me an intense look. "You sent me the package two weeks ago with strict instructions to open it in the event that you became involved with the law, or due to any marital problems. It's like you planned last night."

"Stop talking to me as if I don't exist. I've never sent you anything with those types of instructions." I opened the folder.

"Looks like your signature to me." She spat cigar juice and plucked a ball from a clean bucket. "Or maybe I'm crazy. No pun intended. I didn't mean for it to come out like that."

I looked up from the documents as she cracked the ball. "It's my signature. So?"

"So?" She pointed the wedge at me. "You signed it all away. You're broke if—"

"He's broke if what?" Tuesday sat down beside me. "Jeanette, you never told me you hired a new clerk. He's a cutie pie."

"Nothing to tell," she said. "Ex-con who'll probably be back in prison before the year is out. Damn boy is confused: a Colombian with dreadlocks." She shook her head. "Figure that one out."

"Well, he's a cutie pie. I had to hook it up so I can get

a slice. So what's this about Parrish being broke? He's a long way from that street."

Here I am dealing with a crisis and Tuesday was off somewhere making arrangements for a booty call and to get high. Some people never change.

Jeanette sat on the sofa with us and then lit the cigar. "You're holding a very well-constructed contract. What it boils down to is, in the event that you and Hana separate, due to any negligence on your part, you've agreed to give her every penny you have, every piece of property you own, and your entire percentage of Upscale Pictures."

My jaw dropped.

"Ain't this a bitch! How could you fucking do some bullshit like that?" Tuesday frowned. "Daddy worked his ass off to change our lives. And you gave his sweat and death away for a piece of pussy. You can buy two pussies better than Hana's for five-stinking-ass dollars—on credit. Fucking asshole. That's your new name: Asshole."

"I didn't do that. I wouldn't, I swear." And I meant it...or at least I thought I did.

"I'm sure Hana's hotshot lawyers are preparing the paperwork as we speak." Jeanette motioned to the folder in my hand. "I've been over that thing a thousand times. It's solid. You'll be broke if she goes through with a divorce."

"I never would've done anything like that." I dropped my head in my palms, my fingertips massaging my scalp. "What's happening to me? I swear that I wouldn't willingly and knowingly sign sixteen million dollars away. I read everything I sign. I don't even remember—"

"Here we go with the I-don't-know-nothing bullshit." Tuesday was fuming.

Ever since we were children, it was clear as day when she was really pissed because her jawbones would throb, like they were now.

"Wait one fucking minute! He didn't give that bitch any of my money, did he?" She started punching me.

Chapter 13

"Would you relax, Tuesday?" Jeanette pulled Tuesday off of me and then sat between us.

I said, "I told you about hitting me."

"Shut the fuck up. You need your ass whipped."

"You two are worse than kids." Jeanette shifted her gaze from me to Tuesday. "That's enough. The only way Parrish can get your share of assets is to inherit it in the event of insanity or death. You're not dead yet, and he can't touch what isn't his." She drew on the cigar. "There is one possible out, unless you can convince Hana not to divorce you."

"Losing your money is one thing," Tuesday said. "Giving it away is another. Amnesia, crazy, or no crazy, don't you think for one fucking minute that I'm gonna give you half of a nickel if Hana zeros you because of your stupidity. Daddy didn't die in vain."

I swallowed the goose egg in my throat. "What's the out?"

"Get me those medical records."

"I guess I'm back to talking Hana out of divorcing me."

Tuesday sucked her teeth. "Asshole." Her mouth was as dirty as Rudy's.

"Out of curiosity," I said, "if the records did exist, how would they help?"

"According to Dr. Rodriguez, the reality of your condition is setting in. We—"

"The medicine." Tuesday rolled her eyes at me and then fixed Jeanette with a sidelong glance. "Hana wouldn't tell me exactly what it was for. I knew it was different from the schizo pills he used to take; that's what made me ask."

Jeanette sighed around the stubby cigar. "Parrish is suffering from multiple-personality disorder. Take it easy on him, Tuesday. It's possible that he doesn't know what's going on."

I felt myself shrinking and becoming as small as the golf balls.

"If one of his other personalities assaulted Hana and signed that contract, if we can prove that his condition is authentic, we may be able to save your wealth." She considered me and then turned to Tuesday. "And keep him out of prison."

❋❋❋

Hana sat at the edge of her and Parrish's indoor pool. She fluttered her feet in the water while Shamar Lindsay swam laps. She adjusted her bikini top and then answered the aggravating phone. She didn't want to be bothered by any more callous talk show hosts or reporters. "Yes, how can I help you?"

The caller took a deep breath. "Don't hang up...please." Although Parrish felt miserable, he found comfort in her accent. "I should've done more to protect you. I'm sorry."

"Goodbye."

"Please hear me out, Han."

"Actually, that won't make a difference."

"I would never intentionally hurt—"

"If your aim was to apologize, it should be for what you've done to me. Exactly who were you going to protect me from, you or the other you?"

"I don't know what to think. I'm confused. Baby, you know me." He could feel Tuesday watching him.

"That's where I pulled a fast one on myself. I thought I knew you." She shooed Rudy away when he landed beside her. "I pleaded with you to take your freaking medicine. I knew that something horrible would happen. I told you things had taken a course for the worst when you came home nude. You pretty much dismissed my anxieties and fears." She paused; he could hear her sniffle. "Of course you swore that you had it under control. I'm afraid you don't all of a sudden control mental illness."

"I don't even know what's wrong with me. Jeanette believes—"

"You're sick, Parrish. And as of last night, you're absolutely dangerous."

"Dumb fuck. Dumb fuck. Dumb fuck," Rudy said, stretching his wings.

"Have someone come for this bird," she said, "or he'll be outdoors with you."

"Leave Rudy alone." His heart dropped. "Why don't I know I have a problem? You're scaring me."

"I'm terrified of you." She took in her distorted reflection in the ripples of the pool. "I can't live with this secret anymore. It's possible that you'll kill me in the process of protecting your image."

Rudy watched her with one eye.

"You need stern help. Whoever this Ms. Rodriguez practitioner is you've been keeping a secret, you should consider hiring a better physician. It's evident she's a mere saleswoman if she couldn't see this coming."

His entire body tensed. "Baby...Han, I wouldn't hurt you; not intentionally."

"Tuesday, of all people, actually came over this morning with the same pathetic song and off-beat dance. No one even takes a druggy serious. She has nerve, being your spokesperson."

He held his gaze on Tuesday as the limousine blended into the express lane. He thought about how Tuesday was turning into the one person she hated: Catherine. "I wouldn't hurt you, Hana. It's just not who I am."

"You'll be receiving papers to terminate our marriage. Do us both a favor and endorse them. My life is too precious to risk. You don't have a clue who you are from one moment to the next."

"Awwk, bullshit," Rudy said, and then took flight.

"I'm your husband."

"My husband wouldn't have beaten and raped me."

Shamar popped his head out of the pool, flicked water on her belly, and caressed her inner thigh.

"I had the opportunity to speak with Ms. Rodriguez for the first time today."

Parrish's blood pressure torpedoed. "I *don't*—" He caught himself and steadied his voice. "At least one of us has. I'm on my way to visit this *so-called* doctor now."

"She saw us out last night, but didn't have the chance to introduce herself. She said you had a paranoid response to our threesome discussion. It's scary to know that a conversation can cause you to short-circuit. But what I find more frightening is—" She pushed Shamar's hands away from her crotch.

Rudy looked at them. "Stinkin' slut. Stinkin' slut."

Shamar gave Rudy the finger.

Hana continued. "Ms. Rodriguez thinks that since you can't remember anything, your psychotic personality has been controlling you for the last year or so. That's about as long as you've been having maladjusted behavior. Last night's conversation brought your real personality back." She pushed Shamar under the water with a foot. "In essence I've been sleeping with a complete stranger posing as you, or whoever is on the other end of this phone."

"As supportive as you've always been of me, if I had a problem that serious, shouldn't you have met, or at the least spoken to, my doctor before this morning?"

"You know how secretive you are. You made me promise not to. You had everything under control, remember?"

"Han, I'm going to figure this out."

"There's nothing to figure. I'm a memory. You're going to end up killing someone; it won't be me."

He took in every word she had spoken and analyzed each of them. "Don't do this. I need you in my life. Let me figure this out. You know I wouldn't hurt you, don't you?"

"The Parrish that I married wouldn't, but who are you? And if you're that sweet, loving, sensitive Parrish, when will the monster take over again? Stay away from me. I purchased a gun. I'll use it if you get beside yourself."

"Don't do this, Han, I love you. I'll do anything."

"I packed away my love and tears yesterday when you split my lip and bruised my eye." She hung up.

Shamar climbed out of the pool. He dripped water down her back while massaging her sore neck. "How did he take it?"

"Like expected." She looked over a shoulder with teary eyes and attempted to smile.

Chapter 14

In a matter of hours, my life had changed from a nourishing stream to a raging river of confusion and uncertainty, destined to drown everything in its path. Were there other people inside of me? Is that why I had been completely losing days and couldn't remember things I had done and purchased? "Big Guy, what have I done?" I looked at the high-end office building standing in front of me.

"Haven't you figured out that God doesn't answer questions?" Tuesday said. "You can't remember one time He—" She shifted her eyes upward. "—held a conversation with you. If anyone ever tells you that He held one with them, they're lying."

A breeze caressed my face. "This isn't happening" were the only words I could find.

Tuesday stroked my back to comfort me. "You shouldn't have kept this from me. Your problems are mine."

Our pops was famous for that line.

"I can't tell you what I don't remember." I examined the building again. "I've never been here a day in my life. I put that on Pops' grave. Tuesday, I didn't even know this place existed."

"Don't disturb the dead." She nudged me. "Let's go inside."

"Yeah, I guess we should." I pulled the glass door open. "Some things you don't forget. I don't know what's going on, but I'm not a nut." At this point I didn't know whether I was still trying to convince her or myself.

✪✪✪

A placard directed us to Suite 511. We shared a contemplative silence as we navigated the dull-colored hall. I undid the button at my collar. The air seemed thin. The closer we got to 511, the narrower the hall became.

The door to 511 swung open. "Excuse me, Mr. Clovis." A huge white man wearing a toupee and an outdated plaid suit dwarfed me in his shadow.

I imagined his retarded hands squeezing the life out of me. He and I locked gazes as I tried to remember where I knew him from.

He brushed by us.

"Hey, do we know—" I thought I grabbed his arm, but it felt like an iron beam.

He spun around so quickly, and pinched a pressure point in my shoulder, I couldn't finish my sentence. He crippled me to my knees effortlessly. Tuesday sounded as if her heart would jump out of her chest.

"You should not put your hands on people, Mr. Clovis." He spoke slower than necessary. "It is not nice. Let that be a lesson to you. Unexpected actions result in unexpected consequences, Mr. Clovis." He released my shoulder from his vise grip and left.

Tuesday helped me to my feet. Now my shoulder and jaw ached.

I went to the receptionist's window, rubbing my shoulder, with Tuesday in tow. The receptionist was a charcoal-complexioned beauty, all of twenty-one. She had that college-student-internship glow. She split her mouth into a smile that was as bright as a 100-watt bulb.

"Hey, Parrish," she said, "I missed you. They all missed you 'round here, too." She thumbed through an appointment book. She looked over the top of her rimless frames at me. "Don't seem to know how to return a phone call no more, huh?"

Tuesday and I traded a look. I shrugged. "Is...Ms.—"

"I'm fixin' your favorite tonight. Why don't you stop by?"

I could feel Tuesday reading my facial expression. I leaned against the counter to keep my balance. I felt... sick. "Do we know one another?"

"Boy, stop." She shifted her gaze from me to Tuesday as if I were really joking. "Parrish, what—"

"Goddammit, lady!" I stuck my head in the window. "Don't speak to me like we're acquainted. I don't know you." I jabbed the point of my finger at her, punctuating my words. "I-want-to-know-where-you-know-me-from!"

Her brows pointed inward. "Who the fuck you talkin' to like that?" She shot to her feet, hands on her hips. "Now, I done told you I was sorry for the way I got ghetto at the clinic; I even gave your ass some time to cool out. But you ain't 'bout to come in here disrespecting me, pretending you don't know me in front of your sister. I don't know what the hell is up with you, but you thought I fractured your little fingers before; come out your mouth at me sideways again and we can tear this mother-fucker up. Fuck you and this job."

With her tangled prose and dirty mouth, I ruled out college and intern material.

Tuesday scowled. "Bitch, you can get what you're look-ing for. I'm irritable and in the mood. All he asked you was a simple fucking question."

She stared as if Tuesday were a used tampon; she looked at me even harder. "We been fuckin' for a year now. You had me abort my baby two weeks ago because of your precious *Hana*. Does that explain how I know your triflin' ass? You ain't shit, Parrish. And nice to fuckin' meet you, too, Tuesday." She slammed the window closed and spoke into an intercom system.

As Tuesday stared at me in stunned disbelief, a door to our right was pushed open.

First my chin quivered.

She smiled and took a step toward me.

My whole body started to shake.

Tuesday grabbed me. "Parrish."

She closed the distance. I read her nameplate: *Lucinda Rodriguez, PhD*. I blinked and then gazed into the same exotic face that I had imagined having sex with last night. The same woman who had sat beside me at the play. The same woman who had made me feel tingly when her leg touched mine. The same woman who was at the root of my and Hana's disagreement.

Lucinda Rodriguez hugged me. "Thank you for the tickets. The play was wonderful." She extended a hand to my sister. "You must be Tuesday. It's remarkable how much you two look alike. Parrish has told me so much about you in our sessions."

The foundation of life as I knew it had just crumbled beneath my feet. The office started to spin, and then everything in my world went inky.

Chapter 15

Parrish's unconscious body was sprawled across a leather sofa in the psychiatrist's office. Mentally, he was taking an ass whipping.

Ms. Rodriguez pulled his eyelids back and shined a penlight into his pupils. "Throughout my professional career, your brother has the most complex case of Dissociative Identity Disorder I've ever encountered."

"I'm not sure I can handle this." Tuesday nibbled on her fingernails, thinking. "Can he be cured?"

"This is an intriguing case study." She ignored Tuesday while checking Parrish's pulse. "When a patient suffers from DID, it's common that each alternate personality assumes its own life and history and sometimes gender and distinct behavior, but each alter usually takes on its own name."

Tuesday held on to Parrish's hand, trying to understand the rambling doctor.

"It all makes sense now: your brother's alter calls himself Parrish, too." She chewed on her lower lip, thinking. "It wasn't the primary personality that came to me for help. I've been treating the alter, who was pretending to be the primary, for the last year. Well, up until the point when he refused treatment."

Tears welled in Tuesday's eyes. She held his hand tighter. "Is that why he's telling me he can't remember things?"

"Exactly." She seemed thrilled as she paced a small area beside the sofa. "When the primary is under the influence of the alter, the primary doesn't retain the memories; however, the alter retains both memories."

Tuesday's breath caught. "This must be my real brother because he doesn't remember what happened last night."

"I believe so. But the personality that I've established a connection with is a very clever manipulator who thrives on playing mind games, and he has psychopathic tendencies." She stopped pacing to fully consider Tuesday. "There's a high probability that we're still dealing with the alter and it's lying about its identity to escape the consequences of last night's behavior."

Tuesday's voice was lower than normal. "How did he get like this? Can you fix him?"

"Parrish developed his dissociative state as a defense mechanism against a negative stimuli. It began with your mother—"

"You mean Catherine."

"Yes. It started with her abuse. Parrish created a second person who couldn't feel the pain, who would be impervious to her gunshots, who couldn't see or hear the sexual abuse that you experienced. He created a *super* Parrish, so to speak, that learned to separate itself from the abuse."

Tuesday's skin crawled. She could smell the funky mattress as if it were in the room. *Time to earn your keep*, Catherine invaded her thoughts. *Hit this; it'll take the pain away*. She rubbed her shirt sleeve against her lips, expecting to see a red lipstick stain.

"Ms. Clovis." Ms. Rodriguez touched her shoulder. "Are you all right?"

"Huh? I'm okay. Can he be fixed?" Her eyes were hopeful.

"My job is to minimize the incidents of mental disorder; my objective is to reduce the severity of his condition. However, I'm afraid my efforts are insufficient if he refuses his meds and appointments."

Tuesday stared at Parrish. "Is there a way I can tell when I'm...you know...with my brother or—"

"What hand is Parrish?"

"Uhm...right."

"His alter is left-handed and very prone to murder."

Parrish sat bolt upright.

✪✪✪

My surroundings were obscure and unfamiliar. I must have startled Tuesday because she flinched.

"Glad to have you back." Ms. Rodriguez reached out to me.

"Don't touch me!" I was on my feet now.

Tuesday said, "Chill, Parrish. She explained everything; we're gonna work through this." Her eyes were watery.

"I need air." No lie, I felt like I was suffocating. I

freed another button near my neck while moving toward the door. "I have to get out." As I was going through the door, I heard Ms. Rodriguez say that I was experiencing a mild form of shock and that it was best to let me cope with it on my own terms.

"I can't believe I ever got involved with your sorry ass." The receptionist confronted me in the waiting room.

Believe me, I was entertaining the same thought.

She said, "You ain't nothin' but a mangy dog like the rest of 'em."

"Please forgive me." I went for the outer door.

She blocked my path. Her expression demanded an explanation.

"I'm not aware of our time together. I don't even know your name, lady." From my knowledge, the notion of actually cheating on Hana had never crossed my mind. I could tell that my words had cut this woman because her eyes glossed over and her lips were trembling.

She laughed some; I figured it was to keep from crying. "Yeah, well, come get your shit outta my house—all of it. I'm through being your booty call." She threw her hands up. "You never loved me. If you did, you wouldn't have forced me to kill our baby. You only loved that I was willing to do all that freaky shit that Hana wasn't."

This time it was I who was cut. Those were the most painful words spoken to me since last night. Abortion? Never in a million years would I support any form of murder. I had taken long breaks from Tuesday each time she had had an abortion as if it were a casual exercise.

My anger wouldn't allow me to deal with her. I wanted a house full of children. It would be my way of correcting my childhood. Secretly, selfishly, purposely, I had been trying to get Hana pregnant against her wishes.

Tuesday was now standing behind this torn woman.

I had absolutely no idea what to say to this beautiful woman with tears streaming down her round face. All I knew was that I was suffocating. I wanted fresh air badly. Hell, it didn't even have to be fresh.

She twitched the corner of her mouth and sighed much louder than what was called for. She struggled some while pulling an attractive engagement ring from her finger. "You wasn't ever gonna leave me for her." She put the ring in my hand and closed my fingers around it. "Your eviction begins at six o'clock this evening. If your shit ain't outta my house, I swear 'fore God I'll give it to all the crackheads in the neighborhood. And whatever I can't give away, I'm burning—starting with your daddy's photo album." She turned her back to me.

Tuesday's mouth fell open. Trust me, I felt the same way.

I spun her around. "You have belongings of my pops?"

"Boy, don't play dumb."

Tuesday's face tightened; her jawbones throbbed. "What all do you have in your possession?"

She rolled her eyes.

"Bitch, I see you have a problem with answering questions." Tuesday started taking her earrings out. "Let's see if I can help you talk."

"You ain't said nothin'. I don't give a fuck about you getting indignant."

I stood between them.

She said, "I ain't buying it when you say you ain't re-membering shit. Go on, tell her, Parrish. Tell her how all your family's keepsakes are at my place. And I really thought you was gonna marry me. Not five fifty-nine, not six oh one—six o'clock!"

I read the engraving on the ring: *Parrish & Sade*. "Sade," I called out to her.

She stopped but didn't turn and face me.

"Where do you live?"

"You bought me the damn house; I'm sure you'll find it if you want your daddy's shit."

* * *

"This is a waste of time. How do you even know who to look for?" Tuesday asked as we entered the New Jersey Public Library.

"I don't." I showed her my BlackBerry. "Sade said that I haven't been returning her calls."

"I remember, but that tidbit of information doesn't help us find out her full name or where she lives."

I glanced at Tuesday over my shoulder and nodded. "True. However—"

"And the fact that you haven't called her back isn't going to establish if her house is in our portfolio." Tuesday was antsy, and she kept wiping the button of her nose with a ball of tissue.

I could tell that my sister was craving. I just hoped that she didn't get too agitated and flip the script. She was pure evil when withdrawal was in close proximity.

I said, "Our subsidiaries own at least sixty residential properties; it'll be virtually impossible to pinpoint this woman through our deeds. But you're right about one thing: this is a waste of time. I don't know this Sade character." I sat down in front of a computer. "If there was any truth to it, though, it'll be much easier if we had an address to compare to our holdings."

Tuesday plopped down in front of the computer terminal beside me and sighed. "And you've done a really fuckin' great job of answering my question. You still don't know where to begin at. You don't know who to look for but a *Sade*. Do you know how many Sades are out there? Damn."

I logged onto Google, and then showed Tuesday my BlackBerry again. "Last week I kept getting these strange messages saying 'baby, I miss you; I'm sorry,' that sort of thing." I browsed the menu bar on my phone. "I thought some lovesick girl had the wrong number, which I still do, but I didn't erase the messages yet."

I found the phone number in my phone that the messages had originated from. "If you give Google a phone number—" I typed the strange number into the search bar, "—they'll give you a name and address."

I thought I would pass out again. The color must have drained from my face because Tuesday turned my computer screen toward her.

Sade Halloway
619 Twin Flame
Hoboken, New Jersey 07030
201.341.2929

Chapter 16

Later that evening Sade Halloway enjoyed a hot bath while talking on the phone to a knucklehead who called himself Ball Game. "I asked you not to get all emotional before things even happened between us."

"That's the problem: *things happened*—intimate stuff." He walked the perimeter of a neighborhood basketball court while the remainder of his street team ran suicide drills. "I got feelings, too. Maybe you can switch yours on and off, but mine don't work like that. You're dumping me with no notice, no explanation. What's the deal with that?"

"I'm not breaking up with you 'cause we wasn't never together like that. You knew the deal. We ain't got to part on bad terms, but whatever you thought we had is over."

"Sade," he said, his voice smooth and calculating.

"Ball Game," the coach said, walking toward him. "We're having practice here. You're a part of this team, aren't you?"

"Don't you see me on the motherfuckin' phone, old man?"

When the coach saw violence in Ball Game's face, he threw his hands up and stalked away.

"Look, Ball Game," Sade said, "you're a sweet guy and I was feeling the... You know what I'm saying. I'm taking care of something. Try to understand where I'm coming from."

"Then tell me what I did wrong."

"Nothing. You're cool. This is about prioritizing my life."

"It's somebody else. Who the fuck is he? Somebody I know?"

"All we doing is going in circles; I done told you this day was coming. When I get my shit together, I'll look you up."

He kicked a basketball across the court. "Look me up? I've been reduced to a *look-up*."

Sade's doorbell rang.

"I gotta go." She stepped out of the tub and wrapped herself in a towel.

"I ain't going out like that. This shit is far from over. That's my word."

"Boy, please. Don't piss me off. Now, I done gave you some pussy, but it's time for you to move on. I need my space." She clicked the phone off.

The doorbell rang again.

She popped her head through her bedroom window and looked down at the porch. "Who the hell is it?"

✪✪✪

Ball Game slammed his cell phone against the black-top and hurried in the direction of his car.

"Yo, Ball, you're leaving your—"

"A word to the wise," the coach said, clipping the player's sentence. "I know this is your first day running with us, but that's one guy to stay away from when he's angry."

They both watched Ball Game's car tires leave rubber on the parking lot.

"Come on, Coach, we all can get a little ticked." He dribbled the ball through his legs.

"That little tick is a time bomb in desperate need of anger management. You'd think that five years in prison would've calmed him some."

The player gave the coach the ball. "He did some time, huh?"

"I wouldn't call it time, not for a cold-blooded murder. More like a slap on the wrist. He may be a time bomb that smokes too many of them funny cigarettes, but he's the best player I got."

"You shouldn't count me out, Coach. It's my first day. So who'd he punish?"

"Found out that a girl he had a crush on started dating another guy while Ball Game was away at basketball camp. When he caught up to the guy..." Coach shaped his hand into a gun and pulled the trigger, "...bang, bang.

He caught a break, though. His uncle was a well-respected but crooked cop. He was also one of those high-ranking officers in the Army. Pulled some strings for Ball Game, and he pleaded to manslaughter."

❂❂❂

I was way beyond the point of being confused. I was somewhere in the vicinity of feeling like a complete stranger and those things in *Alien vs. Predator*. Even my hands seemed as though they belonged to something else.

I closed the file of my medical records as we parked in Sade's driveway. "Why would I waste money buying a house down here?" I took in the neighborhood once more. Boarded-up houses. Vacant lots. Dirt yards. Rough-looking kids. Trash-ridden streets. A stray dog with a bad limb. Crack addicts. The ghetto.

"When you're a no-good womanizer," Tuesday said, "you do shit like this to hide it from your woman—especially if she's famous." She gave me a smirk. "Your alter ego brang out the trifling niggah in you." She split her mouth into a wide smile that was everything but kind.

"Don't ever call me that again and don't patronize me." I climbed from the backseat, went to the front door, and rang the bell.

At the house on the left of Sade's, an overweight man was on the front porch barbecuing, staring at me like I was a bill collector. At the house on the right, faded curtains hung out of the second-floor window and Natalie Cole blared from the stereo.

"This isn't my style."

Tuesday climbed the porch steps behind me. "We're a half-hour late. There's nothing burning." She pressed the bell. "That's a good sign."

I wanted to say that there was nothing to burn. Denial was all I had left. Naturally, I wanted to hold on to it. But after reading my medical records, in combination with some unexplainable past experiences, denial wasn't something I could successfully defend. And I still couldn't figure out why my jaw ached so badly.

"Who the hell is it?"

Tuesday and I looked in the direction of the voice. Sade was leaning out of a window above us.

"I...I apologize for being late," I said, thinking about how ghetto she came across.

"Boy, use your damn key and stop leaning on the buzzer like you the police." She shut the window.

Tuesday lifted her brows and shrugged.

I examined my key ring: house key, two car keys, boat key, office key, deposit box key, garage key, and...I had no idea what this other key unlocked. It scared me, but I laughed. "This isn't happening."

"Staring at it isn't gonna help." Tuesday rocked in place. "I have to pee."

The key further confirmed the medical records. The door unlocked.

Tuesday hurried by me. "Where's the bathroom?"

"Go in the kitchen, turn left, and it's the first door on the right!" Sade yelled from the second floor. "Ah... Parrish...c'mere, please."

No lie, I staggered when I reached the top of the stairs. Sade was the upper crust of beauty. Her naked body was extremely dark and curvy. I didn't even know that black folks still came that black. Her patch of pubic hair blended with her skin. Her breasts were ripe and set upright. She held my eyes for a moment and then turned and leaned over the sink to get closer to the mirror while painting her full lips with gloss. The position caused her ass to protrude more. Her pussy saluted me through the gap in her legs.

I turned only my head; nothing else would move. "Could you please put... You should cover yourself."

"You really trippin'. Come fasten this for me."

When I turned back, she was sliding her arms into a bra. She bat her lashes over her shoulder. "You gonna help me or stand there? Even though your sister ticked me off, it's rude for us to leave her downstairs like that."

When I was close enough to smell her, it felt like the Kentucky Derby was stampeding through my chest. Now that I was closer, I could see the tattoo on her left cheek: *Parrish's Ass*.

She faced me when I was done fumbling with the clasp. She stepped into my space and then put her arms around me. "I'm sorry for showing out again. You know how I can get." She paused and took a breath. "I ain't got the authorization to be digging through people's medical records. I probably could get away with it if I put my mind to it. I made it a point not to pry." She rubbed her pubic hairs against my zipper. "I knew you was seeing Lucinda for counseling. She always said that it wasn't nothing serious. I trust Lucinda. I ain't snoop 'cause I trusted you and trusted what you told me as our relationship grew."

I swallowed. "I apologize, but I... What did I tell you?"

She twitched the corner of her mouth. "That you was seeing Lucinda for *depression*. Don't be tellin' lies to me, Parrish. I mean it, boy. After y'all left today, me and Lucinda had a long talk. I don't love you no less."

She was a foot shorter than me. I searched her eyes for a connection.

She said, "At first I wasn't having you not remembering me, but I kinda got an understanding now." She stood on her tiptoes and whispered: "When I give you this pussy tonight, it'll bring back some memories."

"How did I ever get involved with somebody so... ghetto?" I shouldn't have said that. "I didn't mean to say that out loud."

"I ain't trippin'. That's what you love."

"I'm not sure what to say to you or where to even begin." Something was definitely happening internally because I was repulsed and attracted at the same time. I wanted to run like hell, but her eyes were inviting. I wanted to see if I could get away with caressing the skin on her bare ass, but I was sure that if I touched it, Hana would somehow find out. "Here I am in the arms of a naked woman, in a home that I'm supposed to have purchased." I pulled the ring from my breast pocket. "An engagement ring. I'm more scared than anything."

She extended her finger, suggesting that I should put it back where it had come from. "I told you before that I'd be there when she was gone. I love you no matter what. I ain't gonna never stop believing in you."

Chapter 17

Shamar rubbed the steering wheel with his thumbs. He was angry with Hana for denying him. *In time you'll wish you had done me right*. He glanced at her, wondering what she was thinking.

It was probably best that he didn't know.

An auburn BMW slammed into their rear. An air bag socked Hana and knocked the wind from her.

Shamar stumbled out of the car with his fists clenched. The kissing cars made him think of when his daughter and a neighbor's son were tangled together by their dental braces after attempting their first kiss. "A red light means stop. Can't you see?"

"My bad, brother," Ball Game said. "I don't know what I was thinking. Is the lady—"

Shamar landed a solid fist to his jaw. Ball Game staggered some and then rushed him.

"Stop, Shamar, please." Hana was still trying to catch her breath.

Ball Game hip-tossed Shamar. His body made a dull thud when it landed on the trunk. Ball Game rushed again.

Hana dialed 911.

Shamar kicked Ball Game's center mass, using both feet, sending the ball player to the pavement.

"What is wrong with you?" Hana said, pulling Shamar across the trunk.

Ball Game got off his ass with a .380 in hand. He jerked the trigger. Shamar threw Hana to the ground and covered her as six bullets tore into the trunk.

Police sirens were loud and near.

"I can't believe...I tried to apologize," Ball Game said, scampering to the other side of the cars. He could tell that the law was about a block away, if that far. He stood over them and noticed Hana's bruised skin beneath her sunglasses.

"I'm a cop," Shamar said.

Ball Game jerked the trigger again while thinking of Sade.

✪✪✪

The notion that I had considered lasting residency in Sade's unattractive home scared the hell out of me. I had to be mentally disturbed. The place made me feel like I was stuffed inside of a Lemonhead box. Even the framed snapshot of she and I smiling and holding hands did nothing to brighten the ambience. I felt tiny and insignificant as I fumbled through a shoe box full of memories that I couldn't remember.

A single tear ran down Sade's face. Her lip quivered

as she held on to a picture. "Excuse me." She took a deep breath and passed Tuesday the picture. "And this is the ultrasound of me and Parrish's daughter. I called her Paradise."

Tuesday gave me the picture after examining it. Her gaze cooled my temperature. Her eyes judgmental.

I read the date written on the reverse side, just as I had done with the other pictures. "Mind if I use the phone?"

Sade wiped her tears. "You pay the bills, why not?" She handed me the cordless phone.

"If you don't mind, I'd like some privacy." I accepted the phone with my left hand.

"Why did you do that?" Tuesday seemed as if something had spooked her.

"Do what? Are...is everything all right?"

Her color drained. She looked the way I had been feeling.

I tried to touch her leg, concerned. "Are you—"

She pulled away as if I had hurt her and would do it again. That moment was an awkward one.

Sade sensed something piercing our trust and made it a point of clearing her throat. "Don't call your bitch from my phone either. Use the kitchen phone." As I got up, she said, "I mean it."

What I saw in the kitchen, staring out from the cabinet, caused me to go numb, caused my skin to pucker with goose bumps: my coffee mug with the chipped rim. My favorite Garfield mug that had traveled with me since

Morehouse. Garfield looked at me and there was no doubt about his thought: *Parrish, buddy, what in the hell are we doing here?*

I called my secretary's home.

"Hello," she said.

"Andrea, forgive me for calling your house."

"Oh, no, Mr. Clovis, it's quite all right." She paused as if she were thinking of what to say next.

"Everything on television isn't true."

"How is Hana?"

From where I was now standing I could see the framed snapshot of me and Sade looking like a poster couple. "Right now, I'm not sure about anything. Everything is complicated. I need you to do a few things for me."

A few ticks later, she said, "Sure."

"Don't judge me, Andrea."

We shared a long silence.

"Okay, Mr. Clovis." She said that like I had given her permission to let go of whatever she had already convicted me of. "I have no right to."

I could hear the sincerity in her voice. That's how Caribbean women are: thoughtful and forgiving.

"Is that all you want?"

"Check my appointment book for entries this year at February eleventh …" I shuffled through a stack of pictures of me and Sade and randomly selected dates written on the reverse sides. "May sixth and March twenty-fifth."

"Give me a minute to logon."

I paced again.

A minute later, she said, "Um...on the weekend of the eleventh, February, you were scheduled to be in Miami. The twenty-fifth of March reflects Paris, and the sixth of May, you were in Puerto Rico."

I sighed. Confidence shot. Bubble burst. Defeated. My appointment book matched the dates and places of the pictures. "One more thing."

"Shoot."

I gave her Sade's address and telephone number, and told her to find out who owned the property and to call me back.

"That'll take me a few minutes. My home computer isn't as fast as mine at the office. And, Mr. Clovis, you're in my prayers."

The second I hung up the phone, someone started banging on the door. As I walked in the living room, we all watched it rattle under the weight of someone's fist.

"Open this fuckin' door, Sade!"

It sounded like he was kicking now.

"Who you got in there with a fuckin' limo? Open the door. I ain't fuckin' playing with you."

Sade's expression went flat. "That's Ball Game."

"Ball Game?" Tuesday and I asked in unison. I pictured a pissed-off Shaquille O'Neal.

"Yeah, Ball Game." Sade rolled her eyes as she got up, biting her nails. "What did you expect me to do while you was playing house with that white bitch every night? I get lonely. We go weeks without seeing each other," she said to Parrish.

"Hana isn't White."

"Open this fuckin' door."

Sade put her hands on either hip and sucked her teeth. "Don't be defending that ho. She don't give a fuck 'bout your stupid ass, Parrish. And she damn sure ain't Black."

More door banging.

If she would have suggested that I hide, I would have admitted myself to an institution for the mentally ill.

"He doesn't mean anything to me, Parrish."

"Girl," Tuesday said, "from the sounds of it, *you* mean something to him. You better talk to him before he breaks the door down."

"I'll handle it." What did I say that for? I sure didn't feel naturally compelled to handle it. But a man should feel compelled to protect his woman, even if she is a side girl.

Sade put her hand on my chest. "Why don't you take a shower? I'll take care of Ball Game. I like that outfit you bought from Saks last month. Please, don't leave your closet messy. I hate cleaning up behind you."

Chapter 18

Sade stood on the porch. She was inches away from Ball Game. "Have you lost your mind?"

"That's funny; I was thinking you lost yours." He cocked back and slapped her.

The barbecuing neighbor just stared.

He put his hands around her neck and squeezed. "When I'm beatin' the breaks off that pussy, you love me to death." He bit down on his bottom lip and squeezed tighter. "Now it's fuck me? No, fuck you!"

The neighbor flipped his burgers.

She pried at his hands. "Let...me...go."

"Now that's where we ain't seeing eye to eye." He scowled at the neighbor and then put the nozzle of his .380 on Sade's nose. "I ain't letting you go. You leave me, it'll be in a hearse."

Sade fought to catch her breath. Ball Game's outburst terrified her. It completely threw her off balance. She couldn't even recall a time when he had raised his voice at her.

James Brown's "Big Payback" blared from someone's stereo.

She prayed that this was a nightmare she'd awake from. "Please take the gun away from my face," she spoke slowly and clearly.

The door was opened. "Sade—"

Ball Game trained the gun on Parrish. "So, this... faggot...is responsible for your new attitude. You said you wasn't fuckin' with him no more."

❆❆❆

Something bothered Tuesday. All of a sudden, she gave me the impression that she was scared.

"Put yourself in my shoes." I took the box of pictures from her lap. "Wouldn't you like to believe that none of this was true?"

"I need to get back home, Parrish. You'll be okay here with Sade. I'll call tomorrow and we'll...I don't know."

"What's wrong with you?"

"All of that is wishful thinking." She wouldn't meet my eyes. "At this point it's called acceptance. You have to learn to control it, live with it." She looked up. When our eyes connected, she lowered her gaze. "We both read the medical records. This woman has our father's keepsakes, a closet full of your clothes—some of which I bought you. She knows shit about us, Parrish—shit you were sworn to secrecy about. These pictures are real. What are you fighting?"

"I'm not sure. I'm not eager to accept this as my reality.

Dissociative Identity Disorder or not, do you know what this implies?"

Tuesday watched my hands. "That you're a cheating dog. That if Hana finds out about your double life, you can kiss your ass and money goodbye. I don't condone cheating, but you'd better get real good at it until you get your issues in order."

The phone rang.

"I'm going home, Parrish. I need time."

"Why do you keep trying to leave? Check the caller ID; it should be Andrea."

Tuesday looked at the display screen and then answered. I was looking for her facial expression to shift as she listened, but she remained unreadable.

"Okay, I'll tell him," she said and returned the phone to its base. "We hold the deed to this house under our publicity firm."

"Which one?"

"Platinum Book PR."

I sighed. "I'm going to shower."

"I'm leaving."

"Can't you wait until I'm out of the shower?"

We heard raised voices.

I went to the door and pulled it open. "Sade—"

An angry man with an athletic build aimed the business end of his gun at me. "So this...faggot...is responsible for your new attitude. You said you wasn't fuckin' with him no more."

The way this guy hit me with a concrete look, I realized that I would die. I showed him my palms. "Whoa!"

"*It's the big payback*," James Brown shouted from someone's speakers.

For reasons like this I never gave the inner city a second thought once Tuesday and I had escaped Cleveland. I had even learned proper English to effectively socialize within privileged settings, to rub elbows with the upper echelon of class. This was out of my league. I was more content hearing about situations like this on the six o'clock news than participating in them.

"Ball Game, put the damn gun down! He just came by to get the rest of his shit."

I nodded, confirming her statement.

"Shut the fuck up." He mugged Sade's head through the screen door.

James Brown was steadily hooting about a big payback. *How in the hell can he put his hands on a woman like that?* "Why don't you try that on me?" I said, reaching for the screen door.

He stabbed the gun in my direction. "I will put a hot ball in your ass and not think twice about it."

I showed him my palms again.

"He's about six foot one," Tuesday said, walking up behind me, speaking into the phone. "He's threatening us with a gun. Yes, blue, blue sweat suit."

"That's right, motherfucker," Sade said. "The police is comin', with your bad ass."

He slapped saliva from her mouth. "I said shut the fuck up!"

Sade buried her head in her arms; I was pissed that I couldn't help. There wasn't a bright red *S* stamped on my chest, so my black and scary ass didn't stand a chance against his gun.

"You're going to jail." Spite dripped from Tuesday's lips. "Bet you won't hit a man like that."

"Skinny bitch, come out here and I'll smack you in your mouth, too." He backed down the stairs.

Sade found her courage. "Stay the hell away from me!"

He shrugged. "I already told you: it's only one way to leave me." He stuffed the gun in his pocket. "I'll be back in the morning. Have a new attitude." He looked at me. "If you know what I know, you better just be here to pick up your shit." He took off running.

Tuesday stormed out of the house. "I'm going home."

❊❊❊

The two men embraced when they met in an alley behind a local greasy spoon. Moonlight saturated a dumpster packed with sour food. Discarded tidbits of thin-crust pizza, gravy fries, and some other decomposing food painted the ground beneath them.

"I thought my performance would win me your applause." Ball Game could sense his uncle's disapproval.

Shamar covered his face with a hanky and spoke through

it. "You almost shot me." The pungent odor knotted his bowels.

"You said make it look good. If I wanted to shoot you, we wouldn't be in this stinkin' alley 'cause you'd be dead. You taught me to handle a gun well."

"You allow your arrogance to carry things too far. All you were supposed to do was shake her up."

Ball Game picked up a pebble and fired it at a rat eating dinner. "I wouldn't call it arrogance. It's my drive to go the extra mile. She pissed on herself. If that ain't shaking her, I don't know what is."

"That's not the point."

"The point is you shouldn't be complaining; just focus on doing your part."

Shamar remembered how she had rejected him moments before the car accident. "Not a problem. Hana's been loving me since she came to this country. It's everything else I'm worried about." He considered the dumpster. "This shit stinks."

"You know, I've been doing some thinking, Unc. Evaluating my self-worth."

"And?"

"Before I make any hasty decisions, I need to know why Hana has to die?"

"We don't get paid if she doesn't."

"I'm not clear on that."

Shamar shook his head. "Parrish is about to lose all his pretty pennies to her. She'll marry me. But I can't control her money if she's alive, which means you don't get a dime."

"I'll kill her, but I get half or I walk."

"Not only are you arrogant, you're greedy." Shamar straightened Ball Game's collar. "And what exactly makes you think you're entitled to half of anything?"

"I'm keeping your pawns in line. Without me, you don't reach your goal." He returned the favor and fiddled with Shamar's collar. "I should get more, but I'll settle for an equal share."

"About my pawns: Will—"

"My part is taken care of. Parrish and Sade are under pressure." He offered Shamar his hand. "Fifty-fifty."

✪✪✪

The steps strained and squealed as Sade stomped to the top. "You know what, Parrish? You done scorched my last motherfuckin' nerve. You still letting that ho dictate our every move."

I looked up at her, repulsed but attracted. "Saving my marriage is first priority. The Hilton is closer to my house than here."

"That bitch don't want you, Parrish. It's obvious something ain't right at home, or you woulda never started playin' house here."

"There's no need to argue about this." I couldn't stand another argument; she had a point. "Please pack us an overnight bag. I'm not thrilled about this part of town, and I'd rather not be here when your boyfriend comes back."

"I done told you, he ain't my fuckin' boyfriend." She twitched the corner of her mouth and sucked her teeth. "Had I known you'd be jealous, I woulda been threw a man in your face. This ain't 'bout Ball Game; you chasing that bitch. I'm so sick of her interference in our life. I wish she'd have an accident and die."

"You don't mean that."

"Yes the hell I do." She slammed a door. It sounded as if she would kick a hole through the ceiling.

Had I any way of knowing the danger I was about to face, I would have stayed in that filthy jail cell to avoid it.

Chapter 19

A few ticks past ten PM., Ball Game followed two car lengths behind Sade's Honda.

✪✪✪

The acts committed by my alter ego, I refused to accept responsibility for. In fact, I'm not thrilled to be associated with that person, even if I were going to benefit. I found myself standing face to face with an ancient question: Why do men cheat? Last night, when Hana posed this question, I hadn't even considered cheating. I answered her with hypotheticals, information based on an *Essence* magazine article, someone else's experience. When Sade strutted out of the hotel bathroom wearing only skin, I discovered the answer to the infamous cheating question. Even with my life in a precarious limbo, and the risk of losing Hana and millions of dollars, I believed that I could get away with it. Nothing more.

Sade stood in front of me with her legs partially gapped. Her dark, curvy body excited me.

Everything below my belt stretched to capacity.

She crawled to the loveseat on all fours as if she were a black panther on the hunt. Her eyes said sex. Her movements were so seductive, I began to feel my pulse... below...my belt.

"A doctor can't prescribe this." She settled her back against the leather and parted her legs. "Come over here and get your memory back."

❊❊❊

Hana's heartbeat quickened as she rose on her tiptoes to look through the peephole.

Nothing.

She put the phone on the other ear. "No one's there."

"You're scared," Shamar said.

"I'm not."

"Then stop whispering."

"Um...bells haven't advanced to ringing themselves, of course not." She unlatched the door and poked her head out. "It was terribly cruel of you to leave me unaccompanied."

Nothing.

"You're whispering again. Now you know what it feels like it. The difference is you left me for four years, Hana; I left you alone for two hours."

"Of course you'd smear that in my face at a time when I'm absolutely frightened." She secured the door. "It's essential you provide full-time security. Just in case."

"I need you in my life full time. I'm getting old. Let's go to Vegas and do it. Marry me."

Hana screamed and dropped the phone. Someone had attacked her from behind.

❂❂❂

Zina Delancey's soulful lyrics filled our room's empty spaces. Sade's legs were penned over my shoulders. I could still taste the secrets of her garden in my mouth, smell its confection coating my goatee. I squeezed the mounds of her ass. Hana's was nice, but no ass in the world could be compared to a Black woman's.

Sade's dirty language excited me, dared me, challenged me, inspired me. "Please, Parrish, harder. Go deeper, you motherfucker." She twisted her face.

My body responded.

"Fuck me harder. Deeper, go deeper. Get it back, baby. Your memory is in there."

I dug deeper and deeper and deeper and deeper. I wanted my memory and anything else I could find inside her pussy.

In. Out. In. Out. In. Out. In. Deeper. Deeper. Much deeper.

She yelped like she was giving birth.

I humped her a million times.

"Your dick makes my insides feel so good." She raked her claws across my ass cheeks while pulling me farther into her heat. "That's it, Parrish. That's your favorite spot. Remember me now?" She thrust her hips forward. "Hit-it-just-like-that. This your pussy."

Zina Delancey sang out: "*Give it to me, make love to me like you missed me.*"

❂❂❂

He studied the bleached-blonde's mannish haircut from his BMW.

She fumbled through a purse as she maneuvered through the congested parking lot.

He eased the power window down. "Need a light?"

God, yes. "Thank you." A Marlboro dangled from her mouth. "My nerves are blah. You're right on time."

"Sometimes."

She leaned into the window and was rushed with marijuana aroma. "Now that smells good."

"I agree." He drew on the blunt. "It'll do a lot more for your nerves than that cigarette." He offered her the blunt.

She eyed the hotel. "Gosh, I would love to. I better not; I'm on my break. Besides, I only have five minutes."

He shrugged. "That's up to you. You can either ride a good high for the rest of the night, or you can get a light and need another cigarette in the next ten minutes."

"Cruising the rest of the night sounds like a plan." She opened the door. "I'm Dreamer. What's your name?"

"Ball Game." He gave her the blunt.

✪✪✪

"Right there, Parrish." She dug her nails in my back and drew blood. "Fuck me there."

More hip thrusting.

"Jesus, you're gonna... Goddammit, you makin' me come."

In. Out. In. Out. Deeper. Deeper. Deeper.

Zina Delancey's smooth voice reached us. *"Keep the rhythm steady. It's taking over my body, baby."*

"Come with me, inside me, Parrish." She humped harder, begging.

When I felt her insides grip and tug on me, my body stiffened, my sex dance lost the beat. I clamped my eyes and exploded. Her oil well gushed. Together the fruits of our labor collided into a messy ecstasy. I collapsed on top of her. Our breathing irregular but in sync.

I whispered, *"A-*plus."

She licked my ear. "Turn over. I wanna suck the head of your dick while it's sensitive. You always love it when I do that."

✪✪✪

Hana struggled against her assailant's horsepower. She had no idea how she would break free, no idea if she would live. Her life hung in the shadow of a hypothetical *if.*

He clamped a hand around her muzzle to quiet her annoying screams. He steadied her flailing body and then whispered, "Just like a White girl to investigate the unknown. A sister would've never opened the door."

She elbowed him. "Shamar, you turd. My heart is going fast." She hit him. "Do not misinterpret my stock. I'm a Hungarian gypsy."

"I love your accent."

"You make me absolutely ill."

He laughed.

"You find this matter humorous? I thought Parrish... Ugh!" She hit him again and then marched away.

Shamar found her and Rudy in the library. She had her nose in a book. Rudy watched him from the desk.

She said, "Leave me alone."

"Asshole," Rudy said.

"Thank you, Rudy." She stuck her nose back in the book.

"Relax, slim. I was having some fun."

"At my expense. I'm too adult for your immature games. Frighten me once more and the security code will be changed for you, too."

"Don't be mad."

"I'm not."

"You don't sound happy."

"If you would grow up, you wouldn't anger me. Only one day and you've managed to get below my skin."

"Dumb fuck."

Hana grinned at Rudy. "I'm starting to like you, Rudy."

"Fuck you. Fuck you." He stretched his wings.

Her smile faded.

Shamar took the book. "*Push Comes To Shove*. You're taking the part?"

She cut her eyes at him; nothing else moved. "Leave me alone, Shamar. I've been beaten, shot at, I wet my pants, and you thought it would be fun to frighten me."

"Thought you wasn't mad."

"I'm not."

"Sounds like you are."

She snatched the book back. "I'm not!" She counted to ten in her head. "You shouldn't have left me."

"Where's your gun?"

Chapter 20

Ball Game pointed to Sade's Honda. "That's my sister's car. It's been five years."

Dreamer swayed to the beat coming from the car stereo. "This is the best break I've had since I started this gig." She drew on the blunt.

"You're gonna be late," Ball Game said, tapping his watch.

"A few more minutes won't hurt. I wish it was some way to, you know, return the gesture. How about we go out sometime? Next bag of weed on me. You won't be disappointed."

"I'm always game."

She looked at the hotel and took a deep breath. "I know your sister and brother-in-law are enjoying the quiet. They have the whole floor to themselves tonight; some rich guy rented it for a class reunion. They'll start checking in tomorrow morning. And the floor beneath them is empty. It's being renovated."

"I want to surprise her, but that doesn't seem like it's gonna happen unless I sit out here all night. Or maybe you could... Nah, I wouldn't want you to get in any trouble."

"Highly unlikely. What you need?"

✪✪✪

Shamar stood behind Hana and covered her hands with his. "It's simple: point and pull the trigger."

Hana pointed the gun at Rudy and then put pressure on the trigger.

It made a sharp click.

"Suck my dick." Rudy raised the feathers on his ruff.

"I have a good mind to put a bullet in this thing and shoot you for real."

"It's that easy, Hana. Point and pull the trigger. A .357, with a four-inch barrel, will stop the Incredible Hulk." He pulled an identical gun from the small of his back. "Carry the same one myself."

"That one is nice. I prefer that one."

"They're the exact same."

She reached for his gun. "Let me have that one."

"No."

"Well, let me hold it."

"Don't want your prints on it." He tucked it in the small of his back. "Just load your gun, Hana. Point and squeeze. You'll be all right." He slipped his arms into his jacket.

"Hey, what are you doing?"

"I can't do this."

"You must stay. It frightens me to be here alone."

He touched her face. "If I stay, it's forever."

Everything was quiet for a few ticks of the clock.

She plopped down on the sofa and picked up the book

Shamar tossed the book to the far end of the sofa. "Stop avoiding this. I love you, but the distance is killing me." He pulled out a set of Las Vegas plane tickets. "Tonight, either give me my heart back, so I can start living, or marry me."

"But Parrish and I—"

"Can't wait anymore."

She studied the tickets. "You're serious, aren't you?"

He stared.

"Shamar, I'm already married. If we marry, it'll be illegal; it'll be annulled."

"I took care of it. You'll be divorced in weeks. An old military buddy is a preacher up in Vegas. Saved his life. He's gonna postdate our marriage for a week after your divorce." He kneeled before her. "Come to Vegas with me."

✪✪✪

I hadn't had sex that intense since Morehouse. So why did I feel choked with guilt? The longer we cuddled, the more my conscience ate me inside out. I guess I hadn't gotten away with cheating on Hana after all.

Sade nestled her bottom against my sticky groin. "'Member how you said you looked into your father's eyes for the first time and knew that your life would change for the better?"

A cold chill ran through me. To my knowledge, I had never discussed how I had felt or what I had thought when I met my pops. Except with Hana. Tuesday and I protected the secrets of our past from outsiders. One secret we even kept from our father. My heart punched my rib cage. "I told you that?" I worried about what else I may have told her.

"Boy, yes, and everything else," she said, turning to face me, our noses touching, tears flowing from her eyes.

"Why are you crying?" I kissed her water-stained face.

"'Cause...just like with your father, when I first saw you, I knew, too. My whole life has changed since you been part of it." More tears came down. "I love you. Parrish, you mean every—"

"So you're fucking messin' around on me with this lame?" the maniac from earlier said, a gun in his hand.

This was the second time in hours that I had found myself on the wrong end of this fool's gun. I knew for sure that I didn't have enough blessings to escape death twice.

"Don't stop now," Ball Game said, settling onto the sofa facing the bed. "I need to hear you say it, Sade. Go ahead, don't be shy. He means what to you?"

❁❁❁

Upscale's executive jet bolted through the sky at a brisk 350 knots. Its cabin's ambience dim; its scent...delicate.

Tuesday turned away from the window. "Clouds are prettier at night."

"The only planes that never land," he said. "I think

clouds become seductive at night. It's like they're flirting with the moon."

She adjusted her lounger so that she could admire the way his locks framed his face. "You're handsome." She considered asking him how he'd earned the name Silence.

"You must be reading my mind. I was sitting here thinking about how good-looking you are."

She grinned and waved him off. "I'm glad you came to hang out with me. I'm not a fan of rejection."

"A weekend with reruns of *Monk* and TV dinners versus a gorgeous woman and Malibu—give me beauty under the California sun. Besides, I appreciate your energy. You recharged me earlier. That driving range is an energy vampire. It isn't ideal work for me."

"What is?"

"Motivational speaker. Targeted audience: troubled youth. I have this thing for computer software, too."

"Then why aren't you making your contribution where your heart lies?"

"When you're on parole, you work where you can. The Feds mean business." He watched her eyes. "The driving range is strictly a stepping stone. I'll be where I'm going soon enough."

"Okay, I'm cool with your prison history," she said while refilling her brandy glass. "It's a turn-on. It throws a little rough-around-the-edges and a dash of ruggedness in the pot. But there's one thing that I'm curious about."

He raised a brow.

"How come you call yourself Silence?"

About time someone had the nerve to question him about his ridiculous moniker.

He studied her while collecting his thoughts. "It's within the absence of sound that a person hears their literal self. Ultimately, when a person can identify and understand their true self, they realize that the silence being spoken is the language of God. My name acknowledges that I realize I'm a spiritual being having a human experience."

Okay...maybe...it isn't so ridiculous.

"You're not a simple dish, are you?"

He shrugged, noting that she was on drink number four. "Is this a habit of yours?"

She swirled the alcohol. She stared at her partial reflection in the murky liquid, thinking about how Catherine had said *it didn't mean anything*. "I have it under control."

"I wasn't referring to your drinking." He took her glass and set it down. "Do you usually call strangers late at night and fly them across the United States for the weekend?"

"When I'm depressed." Her thoughts shifted from Catherine to Parrish. She knew that he was lying about something. "I'm not traditional. I determine my status quo. I see someone I want, and I get him or her." She picked up her drink and drained it. "Consider me the exception, not the rule. There's no prescribed waiting time. No specific number of dates and phone calls that have to occur before I give in to a decision I've already made two minutes after I've met a man."

"Only two?"

"Give or take. You knew, too. That's why we exchanged numbers. When I saw you in your cute uniform, carrying that bucket of golf balls, I knew. Look, Silence, I wanna have sex with you, feed you, party with you, and have sex with you again—if the first time was good—before the weekend is over. So, I hope you wanna put your spiritual being inside of me so we both can have a human experience."

He laughed. "At least you don't have any hidden agendas to sift through."

"Straightforward and to the point." She crossed her legs, thinking about Jeanette's comment about Silence being a confessed Colombian with locks.

"So, how does this work when the weekend is over? Then what?" he said.

"Then it's over, just like the weekend. I don't come with strings. The memory will be enough if we're satisfied." She poured another drink. "Question."

"Fire."

"Do you usually accept strange women's advances and fly away with them into the uncharted? I could tie you up and keep you captive or something."

"You'll let me go when you find out how much I eat." He licked his lips. "Serious, though, I move with life's suggestions. It's either black or white; haven't developed a gray area. I'm working on it. I'm down with creasing your cheeks. I'm not one to live in the *what-if* factor."

Chapter 21

Ball Game took his key card out of the suite's door. He carefully picked his way through the elegant room toward the voices coming from the master bedroom.

"Why are you crying?" he heard Parrish say.

"'Cause...just like with your father, when I first saw you, I knew too. My whole life has changed since you been part of it. I love you. Parrish, you mean every—"

"So you're fucking messin' around on me with this lame?" Ball Game inched into the room, pointing the business end of his gun.

Parrish clamped his eyes and shook his head in defeat. *This can't be happening.* He would find out soon enough that it was happening all right.

Ball Game sat on the sofa at the foot of the bed. His nostrils throbbing. "Don't stop now, I need to hear you say it, Sade. Go ahead, don't be shy. He means what to you?"

✪✪✪

I opened my eyes. God, I wished he wasn't still sitting there with a deadly toy swaying in his hand. I wondered how they would find my body come checkout time. I found myself showing him the palms of my hands again. "Man, this isn't what you think." I could feel Sade tremble; her skin turned cold.

"Oh really? Shut up, motherfucker. This ain't got nothing to do with you. It's about me and her. But you *will* experience the side effects." He crossed his legs as if we were having a social get-together. He turned his temperature-dropping gaze on Sade. "Finish."

She said, "Come on, Ball Game. I thought we were better than this." She held the sheet across her breasts. "Why are you doing this?"

He fired two shots into the mattress near our feet. I felt the same fear as I had when my mother whizzed bullets by me. I began to pretend that this was happening to someone else.

He pointed the gun at my face. "Tell him or I'll kill him."

Sade had no control of the tears. "You mean everything to me," she said, her voice barely audible.

"Look at him and say it like you mean it."

She faced me, lips and chin quivering. "I love you... You mean the world to me."

He clapped five times, gun in hand and all. The thuds were slow and menacing. "I'm not thoroughly convinced. Throw the sheet on the floor."

I said, "I have money."

"Sheet." He pointed to the carpet. "On the floor."

Four heartbeats later, we sat on the bed with our bodies exposed as if we were about to audition for a porno.

"Your turn. You love her, right? Tell her." He jabbed the gun at me.

I remembered a time when I had watched through a key hole as my mother made Tuesday tell a naked White man she loved him.

"Make no mistake about it, I will enjoy killing you. I said tell her you love her, Goddammit." His voice was withdrawn and calculating.

"Okay, okay, you win. I'm sorry, Ball Game, I shouldn't have called it off like that. We can put it back the way it was."

"Bitch, shut the fuck up! I gave your dumb ass a chance to do the right thing." He shifted his attention and the point of the gun to me. "Excuse her for being rude. She interrupted you, playboy. Slap her and tell her not to interrupt you again."

"Please don't make me do that." I shook my head several times.

He stood, lining his gun with my head. His finger curled around the trigger like I had witnessed my mother's.

I smacked her.

"You're mad! Slap this slut harder."

I hit her with a force that turned her head. "Don't interrupt me when I'm speaking." I said those words, but I hoped that she understood what I had really said: *follow this fool's instructions.*

He clapped and reseated himself. "Continue."

I felt bad for striking Sade. I told her, "I love you, too." It was forced, though.

"You see that?" he said. "Huh, you silly bitch? He doesn't love you. But since you seem to love him so much, prove it. Suck his dick...and...turn around and open your legs so I can see your pussy while you're doing it."

She wept. "I'm sorry."

I said, "Please don't make her do this." I was a nine-year-old boy again, trapped in a room with a stinky mattress, begging the devil to leave us alone.

"Ball Game, baby, I'm sorry. I'm yours, baby. Let's end this."

"Be real: Would you rather die or suck a dick? Your magic number is three. I'll count...slow."

From that moment I knew that no matter what we did in an attempt to save our lives, the outcome wouldn't be good.

He started counting. "Two and a half..."

❂❂❂

"Ms. Clovis–" The pilot interrupted their conversation and spoke over the intercom. "We'll be landing in five minutes. Your limo is standing by."

Silence raised a brow. "You really think that? That's wild."

"Don't kid yourself," Tuesday said. "More men are dogs than not."

"According to your frame of mind. It ain't cool stuffing us all in one box. And because you see the world that way, I guess that's your justification for your random sexual episodes and your refusal to participate in a committed relationship."

"Men have been dogging me since I was a little girl. I'm happy to return the bark. You can't commit to natural-born cheats. Sex is entertainment; outside of that it means nothing. I don't associate feelings or emotions with it. When I'm in the mood for entertainment, I reach into that *box* and meet my needs. I've been hurt by a lot of swinging dicks. I'm not putting myself out there to get hurt all over again. It ain't that easy."

He figured the alcohol had loosened her tongue. "Sounds like your mind is made up."

"We have an understanding then?"

"Look, Tuesday, I'm gonna fuck you since that's all you want."

"Appreciate it."

"But for the record, I don't have time to be creeping under the radar, trying to dodge my woman. If I feel like I need variety, I know how to speak up or say goodbye. I'm not a cheater. If I'm single, I enjoy the amenities of that status. If I've made a commitment, I honor that agreement."

"Sure, smooth talker. You broke the implied agreement that came with me being your date. You couldn't even respect me and not stare at that chick in the restaurant. You wouldn't have lost any *player* points if you had just excused yourself and went and talked to her. I can imagine how disrespectful you'll come across to someone who is your woman."

"Looking isn't cheating."

"No, but it's rude when it's tactless." She wet her lips. "Your date is supposed to be at the center of your attention."

He laughed and studied her, shaking his head. "Men are visual; you can't compete with genetic coding. You'll only become more angry and disconnected with us if you try. But on our part—and I'm speaking for all men who are after a solid relationship—we can't promise to stop liking and admiring chocolate; only to stop eating it."

"Promises." A devious smirk painted her face. She leaned closer to him and traced the sacred OM mantra tattooed on his forearm. "Promise is a word that has lost its definition when spoken from the lips of men. Be real: why do men promise us to stop eating chocolate, vanilla, pecan, and all the other ethnic flavors, but months into the fling, we find out that y'all have dipped or have been dipping your spoons all along?"

He massaged his temples.

She sat back, crossed her legs, and said, "Think of a good lie. Remember, you're speaking for all swinging dicks."

"Lie? I don't owe you a lie. In this case I can only speak for myself, from my own experience with cheating." He gathered his thoughts. "I was young, nineteen years old, and a circumstantial cheater. My relationship had stopped making progress, plus she was sexually boring. At the time I was immature and didn't know how to tell her without cracking her fragile esteem. I met someone who offered me good sex and progress. I took it."

"Scratch the progress part; I'm all in for the good sex."

Chapter 22

What I had been subjected to within the last twenty-four hours forced my existence into a runaway tailspin. Having this fool in close and uncomfortable proximity, watching and encouraging Sade to perform oral sex on me, proved that the spin had gained momentum. I pleaded with God to stop Ball Game from making me return the favor. I closed my eyes. Not because it felt good, but because I couldn't watch her perform and cry in my lap. Plus, the last time I looked down it wasn't Sade at all. It was my eleven-year-old sister with tears.

"That a girl," Ball Game said. "That's how I like to see it: head down, ass up. Open your legs wider. Show me your peach cobbler."

Something…wasn't…quite right with his voice. It fluctuated. His breathing rushed. I peeked around Sade to make sense of the voice. What I saw was not pretty. Ball Game held the gun in one hand and stroked himself to a climax with the other.

I pushed Sade away. "Aw, come on, man. What are you doing? This isn't right. Put that thing back in your pants."

Sade wept. "Please, please, Ball Game. Please forgive me."

He leapt from the sofa. I see why they call him Ball Game. He was at my bedside in one meticulous motion. His baby maker still bursting through his zipper.

"Did I fuckin' tell you to stop?" He spoke to her but struck me. "Tramp, you're gonna force me to kill your boyfriend, huh?" He struck me over the head again. It hurt worse than when my mother had done it. I saw white lightning bugs flying around the room.

He reared back to crack me a third time. I tucked my head in my arms and curled into a ball. Trust me, the first blow knocked the notion of *fight* out of me; I couldn't stand another one.

Sade grabbed his arm before he could lick me again. "You're hurting him. Stop it, please, Ball Game. You'll kill him."

"You'll be joining him." He backhanded her off the bed, sending the gun whirling across the room.

I rushed him.

We tumbled over the back of the sofa and into a bureau. I kneed him in the groin—hard. I bet he wished that he had put that thing away now.

"Stop, goddammit!" Sade's voice came from behind us.

He head-butted me and then hit me with an elbow. He bit me in the chest as we rolled and punched each other.

The gun exploded.

We both froze and looked at Sade. She shook so bad I was sure she would shoot me by mistake.

Ball Game laughed while standing up. "Baby, guns is for grown men. Give it to me." He started toward her with his hand out. He took careful steps.

"Boy, so help me God, if you come any closer, I'll shoot you dead."

I went to her and eased the gun from her. "Call the police."

"You know," Ball Game said, zipping his pants, "for a minute there, I thought I would make the obituary. Sade can be a mean bitch. But I know you're a coward." He charged.

Sade screamed.

I pulled the trigger.

❋❋❋

"I'm feeling this," Silence said, looking through floor-to-ceiling glass doors. "Any time you can walk off your patio and onto a private beach…" He nodded. "Yes, this would be a place to call home."

"You can admire the property later." Tuesday unbuttoned his shirt and began caressing his chest. "I can tell you worked out a lot in prison."

"Mostly my mind." He pulled the back of her hair, exposing the skin of her neck. He ran his tongue from the base of her neck and traveled her jaw line to her lips.

She licked her lips after the kiss. "You got some skills. If your mind is as sharp as this body, some chick is gonna be lucky."

"Lucky you." He pressed her against the glass door and explored more of her with small kisses.

"Stop." She pulled away. "I'll be right back. I have something that'll make us feel good while we make each other feel good."

She was a little thinner than he preferred, but he really found himself enjoying the seductive sway of her hips. He delighted himself with her backside until she was out of sight.

A cell phone rang.

"Is that mine or yours?" Tuesday called out from a guest room.

"Mine," he said, flipping his phone open. "Talk to me."

"I thought I told you to call me when your flight landed."

"Things started heating up pretty fast."

"Just because we're friends, I'm still your parole officer. I have a job to do, Silence. If I ask you to call, call."

Silence heard Tuesday's footsteps. "I'm about to get some. I'll call you back."

"Silence—"

"Tomorrow, Ced." He closed the phone as Tuesday strutted into the room wearing only a thong and carrying a serving platter. He studied her subtle curves. Her erect breasts and flat stomach. The way the fabric of her panties was fitting between her legs. The rich hue of her skin. "You're a beautiful woman, Tuesday. You remind me of a German chocolate cake."

"I sure hope you ain't on a diet." She set the platter

in front of him. "Choose your pleasure. I like them all."

Hell nah! He was positive that his expression reflected his inner feelings. The platter held portions of various drugs: marijuana, powder cocaine, rock cocaine, ecstasy, heroin, and something else he couldn't identify. *This broad is a junkie.* "I don't get down like this."

"What did you think I meant by having something to make us feel good?"

"It wasn't drugs." He buttoned his shirt.

"Let's just smoke a joint together."

"Look, I don't fuck around. And I don't fuck with anyone who does drugs." He stuffed his shirttails inside his jeans. "You flew me out here to put my freedom in jeopardy. My parole officer is cool, but I can't explain this—" He gestured to the smorgasbord of narcotics. "—if the cops come busting up in here."

Tuesday tried to touch him. "Chill out. You said you were down with a wild weekend."

He talked and walked toward his backpack near the front door. "Sometimes my *yes* turns into *no*." He adjusted the backpack on his shoulder. "Not that I don't have the ability to make firm decisions, but my answers change as my awareness grows." *What a waste*, he thought while shaking his head. "I'm fully aware that I'm not down with this party." He opened the door. "If you don't mind, I'll stay in your guest house tonight. I'll be on my way first thing—"

"Silence, you don't have to trip so hard. It's not that serious."

"I'm not trying to hear it." He walked out into the heat of the night.

✪✪✪

Hana couldn't sleep. She left Shamar in bed snoring. She took the elevator to the kitchen, looking to moisten her parched throat. She filled a glass with the last of the grape juice. The refrigerator spat out a detailed grocery list. With the glass in hand, she figured she'd get some reading done as she navigated her way to the library.

Rudy lounged in his airy cage. He watched her with one eye and said, "Stinkin' slut."

"Screw you, Rudy. You're horrible." She removed Shamar's jacket from her chair and noticed it was heavy. "You must learn to guard your mouth if you want to eat. I'm your primary caregiver now."

"Fuck you, fuck—"

"Zip it," she said, throwing a cover over his cage.

She looked inside Shamar's jacket, finding the handle of his .357 poking from the pocket. Remembering that Shamar didn't want it printed by anyone other than himself, she used the fabric of her nightgown and eased it from the pocket. *I still prefer this one more.* She pulled the desk drawer open and then exchanged her gun with his.

She settled herself in her chair and snuggled with the novel *Push Comes To Shove*.

Chapter 23

The gun went off.

Ball Game staggered back a foot. He gazed at the marble-sized hole near his heart while patting it to see if it were real. He shifted his eyes toward me and then collapsed in a heap.

My hand was stuck to the gun handle. I was frozen solid with fear.

Sade's mouth gaped; her eyes bulged. She knelt beside his body and felt for a pulse. Make no mistake about it, when she looked up at me, the horror contorting her face confirmed my worst fear.

She said, "You murdered him." Just like that.

"It... You saw it. It was an accident." An unseen hand turned my world upside down and shook and shook and shook until everything fell out. The life I adored only days ago was no more. "It was an accident. I'm calling the cops. We'll be fine. It was an accident." On some level I believed that if I said *accident* enough, it would make the body lying on the floor go away and would put a patch on my pro-life position. I headed to the phone.

"No!"

I turned to her.

She was on her feet now. She made no other movement. She stayed focused on the gun I had pointed at her.

When I realized what was going through her head, I threw the gun onto the bed as if it were evil. "We have to call the cops."

"Boy, you'd better think long and hard 'bout what you sayin'. This is called murder. Ain't nobody gonna believe this was an accident." She twitched the corner of her mouth. "You done made yourself a pattern. Whether you knocked the hell outta Hana or not, people think you did. You roughed up a camerawoman on TV, now this." She started dressing and tossed me my boxer shorts. "If we call the cops, you'll spend the rest of your life behind bars."

I paced and thought. Every few seconds or so I would peep at Ball Game. My mind told me that I could see him breathing. But the blood soaking his shirt told me otherwise.

"Parrish."

"Shut up! Let me think." I imagined the cops storming the room and taking me away forever. "He broke in here. He forced us to... He assaulted me. He had the gun, Sade. I protected us. They would believe that."

"Are you stupid? He has semen in his underwear." She pointed. "It's on the couch. Don't you watch *CSI*? It's in me, along with yours."

I looked at her hard. I wished that Rudy was here because he would say what I was thinking.

"You ain't got no right to be lookin' at me like that."

She lowered her head, shameful. "I was with him last night. You hadn't been around in weeks. Parrish, if we call the police, they're gonna think this was a lover's quarrel. Look at this through the lens of a movie producer. I broke up with him. That bullshit at my house. Your sister and my nosey-ass neighbor saw it. Now he's dead." She sat on the bed and put her shoes on while she talked. "Given everything that happened over the last day, you're going to jail for Muur-duur." She said it slow and clear.

I guess she figured that if she stressed the pronunciation, the situation would sink in deeper.

She said, "Jail. The pen. Three hots and a cot. Life over. Get dressed, Parrish. It don't take a rocket scientist to know that."

"You know the truth." I pictured everything on the Big Screen like she had suggested and knew that I was on my way to prison. "You'll tell them everything." It dawned on me, as far as my screwed-up memory knew, despite all that I'd learned, that this was a stranger standing before me. "You will tell them, right?"

She downcast her gaze, avoiding my questioning eyes. "Won't you?"

She sighed way too loud. "Yeah, but they ain't gonna believe me and you know it. I ain't cut out for the pen." She pointed to Ball Game. "I love you too much to lose you like this. We gotta make this go away."

"You couldn't have possibly heard yourself. He's dead. How in the hell do we make dead go away?"

She tossed my pants. "Get rid of the body."

✪✪✪

At a few clicks after midnight in Malibu, Tuesday sat in the sand, twenty yards behind her patio doors, with the Pacific Ocean licking her feet. She stared at the light, which speckled the darkness as it shone from her guest house. No one had ever been able to penetrate the security vault she'd built around her complicated life. Not until *him*. For the fifth time, she found the courage to begin dialing his cell phone number. But like all the other times, she wasn't strong enough to enter the last digit. This was not the way she was supposed to feel about men. Nope. No way.

She turned the phone on again. *I hate you for rejecting me*. Up until now, limiting men to sexual objects, which she would discard come morning, had worked. However, Silence awoke things within her that had died when her innocence was stolen on a dirty mattress.

A salty breeze blew in from the north. She dialed his number; this time she followed through.

✪✪✪

A TV, positioned in front of an overstuffed couch with Silence stretched across it, watched him sleep. When the phone prodded his eyes open, he looked at the TV and saw Jack Bauer put a plastic bag over a man's head. He answered on the third ring. "Talk to me."

"I thought about our conversation tonight," Tuesday

said. "I'm still replaying it. It was more personal and pleasurable than any sex I've ever had." She dug her heels in the sand. "Give me more. Meet me."

"I highly doubt it. I'm watching *24*, which I don't miss for no one. Plus, this whole trip was a mistake."

"You shouldn't be like that. Just because we got off to a bad start doesn't mean it has to end on the same note."

"That's true, but everything we've started has already ended."

"Please, stop rejecting me. I'm too brittle to handle it. I'm really trying here. I just want to talk."

He sat up only because a commercial came on.

"I'm on the beach; it's my favorite spot. Just come outside and sit with me."

He watched her from the window for a few moments and then went out into the night. "No more surprises."

"It's all good."

He sat down beside her and turned his phone off. "This is really beautiful. God knew what She was doing when She made the Earth."

Tuesday pulled her knees to her chest and hugged her shins. "Sometimes I come out here and listen to the ocean until the sun rises."

He looked at the water as far as the darkness allowed him to see, thinking of how majestic it was. "What does the water say to you, Tuesday?"

"Never thought of it like that. I wouldn't even know how to interpret what the ocean says to me in words. It's healing. It helps me unscramble my life, make sense of it."

"How often do you come here to listen?" He etched an infinity symbol in the small patch of sand between them.

"Only when I'm lonely; when I'm tired of listening to the drugs."

He thought about that. "Considering—"

"I'm always lonely, Silence." She laid her head on her knees, staring up at him. "I'm sick and tired of listening to the other stuff, too."

"I used to seek contentment in superficial things—money, willing women, alcohol—which all led me to prison, more so the alcohol. I kept waking up in the morning alone, even with a woman in my bed. I couldn't figure out why until I learned how to communicate with life in a different language." He pondered the water. "The language of the ocean. I began to use my heart, which didn't allow me to use and abuse my body chasing a superficial thrill. Everything I was looking for, on the outside of me, I found in here." He gestured to his heart. "I'm no longer empty, lonely, or afraid when I'm chillin' with myself."

"I'm so sick and tired of the emptiness." She took in a deep breath, pushing it out slow. "Show me. I hate the fear. I want to love. I just don't know how."

"It starts with discovering your divine purpose and supporting it. If not, you'll only continue to take away from it. Loneliness is birthed from not being intimate with yourself. Love and happiness begin with you. Nothing and no one else can give you those attributes. Determine your own weather."

She traced the infinity symbol he had drawn. "I wish I could look at the world through your eyes."

"Then you would see a beautiful woman trapped in turmoil. A woman who needs someone to believe in her and encourage her." He touched her hand. "A woman who needs someone to hold her hand while she heals."

Chapter 24

T he morning of September 4th found Shamar in an abrasive mood. He would be even coarser if he knew that this day promised to test him with the most difficult task of his life.

"Damn," he said, jerking the car back into PARK.

"It makes me absolutely ill when you huff and puff for no apparent reason." Hana folded the grocery list that the refrigerator had given her last night. "What aggravates you?"

"Nothing. I forgot something in the house."

"Please be swift about it. There are tons of errands to run before our flight."

He climbed from behind the steering wheel, trotted to the house, while favoring his injured knee, and went inside. He went straight to the desk and turned up the corners of his mouth when he tugged the drawer open and saw Hana's .357. He pushed his hands inside a set of leather driving gloves, removed her gun, and then substituted it with his.

Rudy landed inches away from Shamar. Rudy watched Shamar stuff the gun in the small of his back. "Dumb fuck. Dumb fuck."

Shamar took a swing, but Rudy was much faster than Shamar had imagined. Rudy flew over Shamar's head and found safety on the chandelier.

He looked down on Shamar and opened his hooked beak. "Fuck you."

Shamar unknowingly rubbed his Band-Aid finger. "First chance I get, you're a dead pet. You know that, right?"

"Asshole."

"Sometimes part sinful," he said, leaving.

"Goddamn liar," Rudy called out.

✪✪✪

Hana adjusted her seat belt for comfort as they backed out of the drive. She studied him and had a few thoughts before her focus fell on his shoulder. She said, "What had you left behind?"

"My gloves."

"Who won in the confrontation between you and Rudy?"

"Didn't even see him."

"Lying doesn't suit you." She pointed to his shoulder.

He followed her pointer finger. "Oh shit."

He hit that smack dab on the knob. *Bird shit.*

She folded her arms. "I saw to it that your gloves were in your jacket pocket not two minutes prior to us leaving. Mind telling me what business you had in the library?"

❋❋❋

Silence enjoyed everything that had transpired from last night up until this morning. But, in truth, he'd rather be in the guest house resting comfortably on the sofa. Where he rested now was more uncomfortable than his old prison bunk. Tuesday snuggled against him as if the floor were a Posturepedic. She followed his collarbone with a fingertip.

"Seriously," he said, "let's get in the bed. My back is kicking a dent in my ass." He peeked at his watch. "It's almost seven; I can't take another minute of this marble."

"You must've thought I was joking. There isn't a single bed in my house."

He pushed the hair away from her face. "Come on; it's 2005. Who doesn't use a box spring and a mattress?"

All of a sudden she could smell the funk of the mattress that used to be stuffed in the corner of her and Parrish's room. She crinkled her nose.

He shook her some. "Why don't you have a bed?"

"I don't want to talk about it, all right!"

He contemplated what she said, what she didn't say, and her sharp tone. "I have this poet friend named Rumi. Met him in the joint between the pages of a book. He once told me, 'Things that seem cruel are from deep friendships.'"

"Don't push, please. I can't digest pushy people. Rumi also said something like, 'No one wants help when life is good.'" She gestured to their attractive surroundings.

"We have a mutual friend. That's deep."

"I'm curious about you right now. What does a woman have to have for you to love her?"

"Everything she can't buy in a store. A sexy crotch, cute face, and nice ass aren't worth a thing to me. It's the intangible things that suspend me in a woman's animation."

She straddled him. "Intangible, he says." *Why ain't I surprised?*

"Yeah. Poise, wisdom, spirituality, loyalty, confidence, passion— intangibles."

She leaned forward. "You'll never believe what I did this morning. I can't believe it myself."

A line creased his forehead. "What?"

❂❂❂

Hana aimlessly pushed a shopping cart down the pasta aisle. "This is absolutely bugging me. I don't know why you insisted on bringing me here. I'm not familiar with this place; it'll take an hour to locate my desired items."

Shamar doubled over, clutching the pit of his stomach. He dropped the canned goods he'd been carrying. "Aw, sweet Jesus, I gotta go bad. Knew I shouldn't have eaten that—" He grunted and hugged himself tighter. "Ooh-wee, I can't hold it," he said, hobbling away.

"Hope you have better luck locating a restroom than I'm having with low-fat tortillas."

He turned off the aisle, straightened his posture, eased on his driving gloves, and exited Pathmart. He trotted to a residential street positioned behind the supermarket and then rang the doorbell on an old Victorian home.

❋❋❋

Ace spoke into the phone at his usual slow pace: "No. It does not work that way. The pictures must be delivered like planned." He placed the phone on its cradle and took in the beautiful image on his computer screen. He imagined that he'd won *Sister Francine's Baby*, an oil painting being auctioned on Oasisnovels.com. He really wanted to add that painting to the others he'd accumulated over the years from the Parousia collection. His fingers were so big, he had to type his bid with a pinky to keep from mashing two keys at once.

The doorbell rang.

He pushed away from the computer station. He selected a toupee from one of many mannequin heads and set it on his bald spot before answering. Whenever possible, he avoided showing his bald spot.

The doorbell rang.

He tugged the door open and found Shamar standing there. "I was not expecting you."

"Yeah, well, I'm here." Shamar stepped inside. "Something came up."

Ace closed the door behind him. "I do not like—" He turned and faced a .357.

"Your hard drive. Let's destroy it; the Photoshop and Signature software, too." He led Ace into a room splattered with week-old dishes, pizza boxes, and saltwater taffy wrappers. The computer screen glowed with a fascinating picture of *Sister Francine's Baby*.

❋❋❋

Tuesday wondered how Silence was able to make her feel...mushy, different. She leaned forward, searching his eyes for the answer. "You'll never believe what I did this morning. I can't believe it myself."

He thought about his parole officer. *Please don't let this girl say something crazy*. A line creased his forehead. "What?"

"You told me that I couldn't live for tomorrow without surrendering today. That stuck with me, made sense to me. I fed my drugs to the garbage disposal."

The floor didn't seem so hard anymore, even with her straddling him.

"It's weird. I've gotten high every day since I was a teenager. I've never been sober this long, but I feel high."

"Experiencing life in the moment will do that for you."

"I think you're my fix."

She rubbed between his legs until the male part of him could stand on its own.

"I've been with a lot of men," she said, stuffing him into a condom, "seen a lot of things, been to captivating places, but none are more beautiful than you." She raised her hips and eased the crotch of her panties to the right.

Chapter 25

A primitive Hewlett Packard printed too slowly for Shamar's frayed patience. It did, however, spit out the document that ensured him control over Hana's estate once she was dead. He folded the paper and put it in his pocket.

"Destroy it all." He clicked the gun's hammer back for effect.

Ace sat at the computer. He stabbed the keyboard with a pinky, executing the command. After a few moments the software wiped the hard drive clean. "It is done."

"Are you sure all my loose ends are tied?"

Ace nodded. "Positive."

Shamar poked him in the back with the muzzle. "But there's a hard drive in your head." He stuck him with the muzzle again.

"What am I supposed to do about that, First Sergeant?" Ace cuffed a CD. "I am honorable." He spun the chair around to face Shamar.

Shamar stepped back, keeping an arm's-length distance. "My intention was to let you live and to pay you what we agreed on. But your dishonesty just forced me to change my mind."

Ace dropped to his knees, his hands in the praying position. "Please."

"It's important to remember what you said in the past before you decide to lie in the present." Shamar felt powerful with the huge man cowering. "You said that you always copy your electronic files *in case*. I'm only asking one time, Sergeant: where's the disk?"

Ace nodded in the direction of the bookcase, which was covering an entire wall. "Second shelf, inside of *Fool, Stop Trippin'*."

When Shamar glanced at the book, Ace made his move. He fired the CD with the precision of a Chinese Star. *Everything is a weapon, First Sergeant.*

Ace would love to murder Shamar. Shamar looked identical to the kid who had tortured Ace in a Utah orphanage. While Ace would be asleep, the kid would set fire to his toes and crush his fingers with pliers. On a rainy morning in 1975, the kid was found in bed with his neck broken. Ace's bed was found empty. Five years later, Ace enlisted in the armed services and knew that the kid had come back to haunt him when he looked into the face of First Sergeant Shamar Lindsay.

The CD sliced into Shamar's wrist. He jerked and shot the computer screen.

Ace pushed off his knees and swallowed Shamar's hands in his. He disarmed Shamar effortlessly. "I am enthused about this opportunity to break your neck again." He kicked Shamar into the bookshelf. "Let that be a lesson in self-defense." He picked up the gun and then dumped the bullets on the floor. "Now it is fair." He tossed the gun at Shamar's feet.

Shamar regained his bearings. He pulled *Fool, Stop Trippin'* from the shelf and found a disk labeled *Parrish Clovis* inside. "Looks like I got myself a rematch." He stuffed the book in the small of his back and then charged.

Ace stepped to Shamar's left and used Shamar's momentum to slam him into another wall.

The impact dented the wall.

A Parousia painting fell on Shamar. *I have to break this big motherfucker down.* He broke the picture frame. He armed himself with the two longest stretcher sticks.

"You can do better, First Sergeant."

Shamar did a front roll and delivered a series of blows to Ace's knees.

"I am not the one with bad knees." He thrust a knee at Shamar's head.

Shamar formed an *X* with the stretcher sticks, blocking the blow. He countered with a kidney shot.

Ace winced.

Shamar had found the giant's weak spot.

❂❂❂

Tuesday bounced on top of Silence. Sweat moistened their bodies.

She maintained eye contact as if she were in a trance. "You feel like God, touching my insides." She turned around, straddling him backward, resting her palms on his thighs. "Spirituality is a journey...You said that." She bucked against him harder.

He enjoyed watching her ass from this position.

"Take me there. Take me on a journey, Silence. Ooh, show me what it feels like to have an orgasm in heaven."

He held her hips and began to drive her to her destination. "You're—"

"Shh!" she hissed. "Please don't say anything. Let the language of God take us there."

✪✪✪

Ace lunged with an elbow.

Shamar flinched. *He's stronger and faster than he was fifteen years ago.* Pain shot through Shamar's body when the elbow smashed into his collarbone. Shamar delivered a knee to Ace's thigh and then shot a fist to his jaw.

Ace smiled. His dick started to swell.

Shamar fired again, determined to knock the grin from his face. Ace slipped the punch, spun and hit Shamar with a back kick, sending him into the computer.

He spotted a bullet near Ace's feet. "Enough of this shit. I'm 'bout to beat your big ass."

Ace charged.

Shamar pushed off the desk, slid through Ace's legs, snatched up the bullet and then hit Ace with two round-house blows to the kidney.

Ace dropped to his knees.

"That's right, white boy," Shamar said, slipping the bullet into his mouth. "Have a seat." He put Ace in a rear-neck choke hold; it felt as if he'd wrapped his arms around a tree trunk. "Go to sleep. I should bite your ass."

Ace pistoned an elbow into Shamar's injured knee.

"Ow! You rotten motherfucker."

Ace pivoted and fell back on Shamar. Shamar used his free leg to deliver a barrage of kicks until Ace let him go.

He jumped up and front kicked Ace with the injured leg. "It doesn't hurt as bad as you think," he lied. It was killing him.

They rushed toward each other, exchanging a flurry of punches and blocks in close-quarter combat.

Ace backhanded Shamar, then wrapped him into the signature move—the guillotine. "It is time." His dick got rock hard.

❁❁❁

"Yes, yes, my insides...here I come," Tuesday said. "Don't hold back."

Silence pushed and pushed until their bodies shook involuntarily.

❁❁❁

"It is time." Ace squeezed.

The first thing to go was Shamar's air. Then the crushing pressure began.

"This time I will make sure you do not come back to torment me." He applied more pressure.

Shamar tucked his chin and turned into the death lock and bit until his teeth met.

Ace roared. His arm went limp. Shamar hit him with a sword strike to the baby-maker. He followed with a head-butt that crunched Ace's nose.

Ace fell onto his back, clutching his groin.

Shamar stood over him and spat the chunk of bicep in his face. "You got excited too soon. How the fight ends is what counts."

Ace made it to his knees. Shamar pulled the book from the small of his back, jerked Ace's head back and crushed his esophagus with the book's spine. Blood drained in Ace's throat. He made a guttural sound while choking.

Shamar loaded Hana's gun, shot Ace in the bald spot, and left the murder weapon with the body.

❂❂❂

Shamar limped onto the produce aisle where he found Hana weighing a bundle of grapes.

"Feel better?" she said, noticing the blood on his wrist.

"I'll feel better when we land in Vegas tonight and you become Mrs. Lindsay."

Chapter 26

"If I were you," Hana said to an African-American cameraman as she walked into the library, "I wouldn't stick my finger in there. Rudy bites."

"Ow!" he yelped, snatching his finger from the cage. "That hurt."

"Asshole," Rudy said.

"He also has a bad mouth." Hana tossed a cover over his cage. "If I don't cover him, you'll have to bleep out the entire interview." She sat down in front of Kimberly Newton, a reporter for *Access Hollywood*.

Kimberly looked at the cameraman. "Take your finger out your mouth. We're rolling in three." She held up fingers and then began the countdown: "Three... two... one." She smiled. "Tonight we're in the home of Emmy-nominated actress Hana Kaffka. For the first time since her September second assault, she speaks about the tragedy and decries her fairy tale marriage with picture mogul Parrish Clovis." She turned to Hana. "Why?"

She swallowed and took a breath. "My union with Parrish was only beautiful on television and in print media. In reality it was the pits. Parrish has mental issues, and he's devoted to keeping his condition a secret. In doing so, I've lived in his prison. I've lived in constant fear."

"You described him as a man with mental issues; would you be more specific?"

"Parrish has a history of schizophrenia; however, a physician has recently diagnosed him with Disassociate Identity Disorder."

"This must have affected you." Kimberly threaded her hands together and leaned forward. "When was the first sign that something was wrong?"

"Um...well, in hindsight, there were many signs. I, however, ignored the red flags. One incident particularly stands out: It occurred two years ago. I'll never forget it because I thought I would die. Parrish has this Garfield mug that he's immaturely attached to. It has a chip on the rim. I looked across the table and saw that he was cut. There was so much blood, it turned his coffee a funny color. All I did was, you know, tell him he was cut. The next thing I know, I was on the floor. He was on top of me, choking me. Blood dripped from his mouth onto my face. He screamed over and over for me to let him out of the closet."

"Were the police notified?"

She shook her head. "When you're an actress, it's difficult to maintain a private life. I preferred that our situation remain in-house."

"But there are other incidents that weren't reported as well. Hana, here's a sensitive question: were you an enabler to your husband not getting professional help?"

"Absolutely. By my not coming forward, I feel as though I helped his situation grow out of control. The first time I contacted the authorities, Parrish had gone missing. He came home that morning nude."

"How has your personal life affected your career?"

"Well, when things became really terrible, I started turning down scripts. I haven't worked in two years because of the stress." Hana's mouth split into a smile. "I've been cast as the leading lady in *Push Comes To Shove*. Filming starts next month."

"I hear rumors that your divorce proceedings are final."

"Court wasn't necessary. Our terms of separation were already spelled out in a contract between him and me. My lawyers only need him to sign the divorce papers. Unfortunately, he's missing again."

"You were spotted in Las Vegas last week with a male companion. Sources tell us that he's your new love interest."

"Shamar? Heavens no. He's my friend and bodyguard. He thinks he's my big brother, of course." Hana glanced toward the back of the room at Shamar.

"Tell us about the night that brought your marriage to an end."

Hana's smile faded. Water flooded her eyes. "He beat me and raped me. Each time he hit me, he would call me Catherine." She blinked the tears loose.

Kimberly handed her a tissue. "Why Catherine?"

"She's his mother."

✪✪✪

A terrorist of Arab descent, with a bomb strapped to his chest, raised an assault rifle.

I squirmed and clamped my eyes. My heart galloped faster than the Kentucky Derby.

He pulled the trigger. Gunfire ricocheted in the cramped room. Screams of death followed the volley of bullets.

"Turn it off," I said, covering my ears. "Turn it off right now!"

"Boy, this my best part."

"Goddammit, Sade, turn the fucking TV off. I can't watch it."

She clipped the screams of death with the remote. "You trippin', you know that? Let it go. What's done is done. You been laying up in this bed two weeks. I'm surprised you ain't got no bed sores. You got an afro on your face; you barely eatin'." She threw the remote down. "And you stink."

"Leave me alone." I turned my back to her, glanced at Garfield, who was staring at me from the nightstand, and then pulled the covers over my head. I heard her suck her teeth and stomp away. But I knew that Garfield was still there. I couldn't remove the image of Ball Game's dead body from my head. I'd lost at least twelve pounds trying to get the image out. I wished it had been me lying on that floor with blood pumping from my chest.

After Hana's interview had aired last week, I couldn't face anyone. But after Conan O'Brien, Jay Leno, and David Letterman made me the laughingstock of America, I lost the desire to keep going. I considered suicide but lacked the guts to follow through. I hoped that if I could lie here long enough, one day I would close my eyes for good.

"Get the hell outta my bed." Sade snatched the covers off of me and then doused me with a pail of water. "And get your funky ass in the tub."

Garfield looked at me as if he agreed with her.

Traitor.

✪✪✪

Sade jumped into my arms when I came downstairs the following afternoon. "That's my baby," she said, rubbing my clean-shaven face. "You look good."

A horn blew outside.

She sucked her teeth and then let out a gust of air. "I hate it when people do that. I don't respond to horns." She parted the curtains. "My damn bell works." She stared. "It's a cab out here."

"I ordered it."

She faced me, brows pointed inward, confusion etched in her face. "Where you going?"

I couldn't look at her. I focused on my pleated slacks and Italian shoes instead. "I can't continue this any longer. I need some time to collect my thoughts."

"That's bullshit and you know it." She was in my face now. "You going to her, ain't you?"

I studied my shoes.

The horn blew.

She shoved me. "Answer me!"

"Yes."

"You bastard." Her eyes narrowed to rivets. "I can't even believe you."

I had already thought about what I'd say to her once I came face to face with this confrontation. Actually, from the moment she had soaked me with that cold water, I'd rehearsed it about a thousand times. "This isn't me. None of this is what I'm about." I gestured at my surroundings. "I can't remember anything. I've gone against every moral I stand for: I've murdered a man; I slapped you, even though it was by force; and I encouraged your decision to terminate our child. I can't take any more of this. I have to repair the life I remember." It didn't come out quite like I'd planned, but it was close enough.

"And what about me? What about our life? You killed Ball Game. I'm the one risked my life to help your square ass cover it; not that cracker bitch, Hana. Don't that count for something? Tell me to my face it don't."

Ball Game burned into my head again. "Right now, all it means is that if you tell, we're both going to prison."

She slapped me so hard that first my face stung, and then it grew hot. After that, it went numb. She jumped back in a boxing stance, pumping her small fists. "Come on, we can fight in this motherfucker. I ain't scared."

I went to the door. "And Hana isn't White," I mumbled under my breath.

"Fuck you, Parrish. You forced me to kill my baby and now you're just gonna leave me."

I froze. That hurt. But like she had said last night, I had to let go. I opened the door.

"I swear 'fore God, if you leave, you better take your fuckin' shit with you."

"I'll come back for it." The sun hit my face, promising a new beginning.

"Uh-uh, fuck that. The hell if you will."

I heard bumps and thumps as I went down the porch steps.

"Take this shit."

Framed pictures of me and her whizzed by and landed on the dirt lawn. I kept going until my pop's photo album hit the dirt. I picked it up and then climbed into the cab.

"Angry women are dangerous, brother," a Hindu man, wearing a turban, said as he flipped the fare lever.

The upstairs window was opened. Out came three of my suits. "Get your shit!"

"Where to?" He smiled at me through the rearview mirror.

"Home... I'm headed home." I smiled, too.

Chapter 27

Our neighbor's loudmouthed Rottweiler ran the length of their fence. It roared and snarled at me as I walked up the drive.

I kicked at the fence. "Shut up with all that noise." I hated that dog just as much as it hated me. On second thought, I hated it more. All it did was bark. *I swear if I could do something to permanently quiet this mutt and get away with it, I would.*

I typed in a security code for a keyless entry; the system denied me access to my front door. My key didn't work, either. I began to feel the same way I obviously made Jehovah's Witnesses feel whenever they rang my bell: unwelcomed.

I rang the bell anyway. I looked up to pray that everything would go smooth and noticed that a security camera had been installed. That irritating loudmouth wouldn't stop. "Would you shut up!"

❋❋❋

Hana and Shamar watched Parrish from a TV monitor. Hana turned her back to the screen. "I'll see him now."

✪✪✪

When the door opened, I didn't expect to be standing face to face with a human totem pole. He forced me against the brick fronting of my home and commenced to searching me.

"Hey, be easy, man." I tried to look over my shoulder, but he forced my head forward. "Who are you?"

He stepped away. "Ms. Hana is having brunch on the sundeck. She'll see you there." He nudged me.

As we went inside, a strange feeling came over me when I was able to get a good look at this man. "I know you."

"Wrong guy." He nudged me harder. "This way."

I stood my ground. "This is my house and I know my way around it. I demand to know who you are."

He socked me so quick and hard, I thought I would either vomit or crap my pants. He put me in some type of chokehold that immediately cut off my air supply. I knew that my arm would break if he applied any more pressure.

He socked me again. "That's for hurting Ms. Hana." He hit me in the same place a third time.

I grunted.

He said, "I don't fuckin' answer to you. I don't repeat myself." He tightened his grip on my neck, or maybe I was becoming weaker. "I don't like you, and I'm looking for the slightest reason to injure you permanently."

"Nice of you to introduce yourself to my bodyguard." Hana leaned against the threshold of the entrance hall.

"Release him, Shamar. I'm certain he understands your point."

I fell to my knees, gulping down as much air as possible. It wasn't until now that I realized how I'd taken air for granted.

Shamar lifted me to my feet. "This way." He shoved me.

When we reached the sundeck, he pulled out a chair at our brunch table. "Have a seat," he said sharply.

An assortment of warm food and freshly cut flowers graced the table.

Hana strutted in like Queen Elizabeth. "This visit is unexpected." She prepared my plate and set a glass of white wine in front of me. She sat across from me.

No sooner than I thought about him did I hear Rudy flapping his heart out. He always tried to cover more distance than his short burst of flight would allow. I held my arm out for him.

He landed. "Asshole."

"I miss you, too." I stroked his coat.

"Dumb fuck."

"For once I think you're on to something."

"When you leave," Hana said, "take him with you. He is absolutely rude. No one can even feed him because he bites."

"I'm hoping I won't have to leave." I turned to Rudy. "I'll talk with you in a minute, buddy." I urged him into the air.

"I need you to endorse this." She pushed an envelope across the table toward me.

My mouth went dry. I knew exactly what was inside the envelope. "I don't want a divorce, Hana," I said between sips of wine. "Can't we talk about this in private?"

"You no longer have the privilege to be alone with me." She glanced at Shamar. "Imagine him not being here."

I could feel him inches away from me. "I find that quite hard to do with him breathing down my neck."

"Either get your closure, Parrish, or Shamar will show you to the door."

I pounded my fists on the table. "I know exactly where my damn door is, Hana!"

She jumped and dropped her fork. Shamar was practically in the chair with me. I had frightened her; that was clear.

I said, "I apologize. I'm frustrated. I can't make sense of anything. But I will never hurt you."

She wiped the makeup under her eye away with a napkin. She was showing me hints of a black eye. "Take a good look. If this isn't a great example of your hurting me, then I'm terrified of your definition of hurt. You only had to take your medicine. Had you complied, my face wouldn't look like this. Shamar wouldn't be breathing down your neck, either." She began eating again.

Shamar cracked his knuckles in my ear.

"Listen, Hana, I'm lost right now. I came to ask that you not turn your back on me. I need you in my life." I emptied my glass. "We made a promise to God to be in each other's corner through it all. This is a difficult time for me." I thought about her interview. I could hear the second hand on Shamar's watch. "How was I supposed to know I needed medication if I didn't know I was sick?"

A tear stained her face. "My primary goal was to be a good wife and cope with your illness." She wiped her mouth, then laid the fork down. "After your behavior, you've made that virtually im-possible. There isn't an accurate way for me to know whom I'm even speaking with now."

"Look at me. You know me. Look in my eyes, Hana. If you don't see the man you trust and love, I'll get in my car and go."

She stared at her plate.

"No, look at me. You said I kept you away from my doctor, and that I did everything my way because I had it under control. Let's do it together. Hell, let's do it your way. I want to repair my life, but I need my wife to help me do it."

"Parrish, how do I know—"

"Because I love you. You know that." I attempted to stand but Shamar pushed me down in the seat. This guy took his job way too seriously. If I had thought for one minute that I could've given him a run for his money, I would've sucker-punched him. *Maybe he looks like somebody I saw on TV*. "Give me one chance to correct this. If it's not to your liking, I'll sign this." I put my hand on the envelope.

We exchanged a long quiet, with the exception of Shamar's ticking watch.

She said, "Under one condition."

"Anything."

"Sign yourself into a mental hospital. When they release you, you may come home. You can take a guest room for the night. My personal affairs aren't your concern until we cross that road again. I'm agreeing to this based on my heart, not my better judgment."

I sighed. "There's something you should know. I've been seeing this woman named Sade."

"You slept with her?"

I felt lightheaded. I could hear loudmouth barking in the distance.

"Are you sleeping with her, Parrish?"

"Give me a minute." I came down with the chills. My food wasn't agreeing with me. "I'll tell you everything. Just give me one minute." Well, I wasn't going to tell her that I had murdered a man.

Chapter 28

The cell phone refused to stop ringing. I felt foggy, as if I were lingering in a haze. I found myself inside my car, parked beneath an underpass. I put the phone to my ear. "Hel...Hello."

"So that's how it is, motherfucker? You just gonna walk out on me for that bitch. So what, she been in a couple of movies. They wasn't even good. She don't even care about—"

"Sade, please, not now. What the..." The glaze over my vision cleared. There was blood on my steering wheel. My clothes. My hands. I looked in the rearview mirror; blood covered my face.

"How you gonna use me like I don't mean shit? You foul."

I turned on the interior light. "Oh God. Oh God." I fumbled with the door handle. "Oh God." I couldn't get out fast enough.

"God ain't got a damn thing to do with this."

"He's dead, Sade. His head is...oh God, Sade. The head, it's on my front seat."

"Who...boy, what you talking 'bout?"

I backed away from the car, still looking at it. "My neighbor's dog. I killed it."

A car horn blew. I looked into the charging headlights of a semitruck that was moving much too fast to miss me. I dove for my life. Guess I didn't really want to die after all.

✪✪✪

The house was empty. Perfect. Hana was probably out having her nails manicured. Now I could get rid of these clothes and not have to explain the blood.

Rudy perched on a settee lining the entrance hall. "Don't trust the bitch."

"Not right now, Rudy," I said, moving toward the elevator that opened in our bedroom.

"Dumb fuck," he said.

I soon discovered that the elevator was shut off from upstairs. For the life of me I could never figure out why Hana had found it necessary to do that. What was the point of having it?

I started up the steps.

I heard laughter.

When I reached the second floor, the laughter changed to panting. It came from our bedroom. The door was cracked. But from where I stood, I couldn't see directly into the room. The closer I got, the more distinct the sounds became. When I peeped through the crack, everything good in me eroded. It was the ugliest thing I'd ever seen.

Hana was on her hands and knees; Shamar was killing it from the back. She moaned and made facial expressions that I had never heard or seen. I gasped too loudly, or maybe they heard my heart as it hit the floor, because they both looked at me.

"Shut the door," Hana said, rotating her hips, biting her lip.

I staggered when another naked man appeared in the door.

"We're busy." He shut the door and locked it.

I kicked and banged and cried. "Why are you doing this?" More banging. "Come out...please talk to me."

"Go away. You destroyed the opportunity to be a part of my fantasy. Just go away, Parrish. You're interfering in my personal affairs."

My palms and forehead were against the door. Tears leaked from my face. She whined and moaned in pitches she'd never reached for me. I pictured what they were doing to her.

My tears dried instantly.

My hurt and pain changed to anger.

My love changed to hate.

I darkened.

I punched the door. "Fuck you, Hana! Fuck you, you nasty whore." I pounded both fists. "You will not disrespect me...not in my house. You will pay for this."

✪✪✪

Silence skipped a stone across the ocean's surface. "You know your brother needs you. What I don't understand is why you aren't in Jersey with him."

"I'm scared," Tuesday said.

"Of what?"

"Him."

"Come on; he's your brother."

"I searched for signs of Parrish but didn't see any." She studied the horizon.

"Maybe you didn't look in the right place."

"It's like he committed an innocent crime. He can't remember, because he's not aware that his other personality has done something wrong."

He skipped another stone. "If that's true, then you have a responsibility to the other people who could be in danger."

"Stay with me a while longer."

"A weekend turned into two weeks. Jeanette is pissed, and my parole officer—"

She kicked water on him. "Are you telling me no?" She ran away from him, laughing.

He ran behind her. "You think that's funny, huh?"

She splashed him and laughed. "Sure do." She backed away as he came closer. "You're kind of cute when you're wet."

"You can't run forever."

"Jeanette's in business because of Parrish and me. She

won't piss me off. I'll get you the year off with pay, if you'll stay."

He frowned and pointed.

She turned in the direction of his finger. "What?"

He grabbed her and pulled her into the water. "I can't believe you fell for that."

"My dress, Silence."

"It's only clothes." He pushed the wet hair away from her face. "Now we have something in common."

She smirked.

"We're both cute when wet." He put his arms around her. "I think you should be in Jersey with your brother. But I'll stay here with you as long as you need me."

"Thank you," she said, slipping her arms from the sundress, exposing her taut breasts. "I want you to stay forever."

✪✪✪

Sade knelt beside the tub wearing a pair of shorts that literally showed off her butt cheeks. "Damn, boy, stand still. You need to calm down." She plugged the tub and then began to fill it.

"She blatantly disrespected me in my house."

"Take these filthy clothes off." She unbuttoned my shirt. "A bath will help you relax. Soak and tell me everything, starting with waking up in the car."

A minute later, I was submerged in the water. I gave her the backstory on all that had transpired since I had left in that taxi. I felt a deep disgust and a penetrating anger, but talking about it eased the tension. All of a sudden Sade started crying. My body tensed. "Did I say something wrong?"

She sobbed even harder. I thought she would hyperventilate.

I climbed from the tub and wrapped her in my arms. "Where did these tears come from?"

"Why can't I be special to you?" She sniffled. "I wear your favorite colors, fix your favorite foods—everything, Parrish. I bend over backwards showing you how much I love you. You refuse to love me back."

"Not right now. Please don't put this on me now. I'm going through things I don't understand."

"Run." She wiped her eyes. "You do that better than anything. You drain me, and then abandon me." She kicked my clothes. "You use me. You only came back here 'cause she dogged you and you knew I'd be waiting with open arms. Soon as you get straight, you're gone. That all I'm good for? Fuck me, eat my food, and then leave me with empty promises." She cried. "All I ever wanted was for you to love me back. The least you could do is try. Stop running from us."

I didn't know that I had been taking advantage of her feelings. I wouldn't want someone I loved to misuse me, either. Back in high school I had ignored Erienne's affections for another young lady I wanted so much to notice me, which she never did. My pops was an intuitive man. He always knew what was going on with me and Tuesday by merely glancing at us. One afternoon, after I had made an excuse to refuse Erienne's call, my pops sat down beside me with the cordless phone in hand.

He had said, "Parrish, every man has a crown jewel that shines only for him. Stop searching for another jewel to polish, cultivate the beautiful crown jewel you have." He gave me the phone. "Erienne is a special girl. She's your crown jewel. Trust your old man. Call her."

Man, was he right. She turned out to surpass special. She's my best friend until this day. Our career choices separate us by continents. Had they not, we would have been an item. This web wouldn't have me snared.

I kissed Sade's tears. It was then that I decided to accept and cultivate the jewel in her. It was the only flicker of light that bore witness that the darkness hadn't yet demolished me. "I'm through running."

She pressed closer, her face against my chest. "I can't be her. I ain't even gonna try to be nobody but me."

"Shush," I said. "I do love you."

She looked into my eyes as if there were meaning written on the backs of them. "Promise me."

"Promise," came out of her mouth easy and automatic. The way an intimate friendship would provoke it. The mirror showed me her shape. I saw my name peeking from the bottom of her shorts. "You and I. Promise."

Chapter 29

I had suffered two blackouts within the past four days. Once Sade had to take off from work to bail me out of jail for indecent exposure, I started taking the medication. I was even having bad dreams of Ball Game again. I wouldn't return Jeanette's calls or text messages. Tuesday wouldn't take my calls. "She needed some *time*" was the message she had had Silence, the public servant guy from the driving range, give me. I knew good and well that Tuesday was hiding in her reclusive suit of armor. Just as she always does when life pitches her a problem she can't effectively deal with, her solution was to drown the problem in drugs or sex.

I was hanging up the phone when Sade came in from work.

She plopped down on the sofa beside me. "I missed you." She kissed me. "Who was that?"

"My secretary," I said, looking at the phone. "It's happening... In a week I'll be financially castrated. My lawyer left me a message with Andrea. I signed that contract during a period when I was considered stable and competent. Hana will get the money; I'll have to prove in a long, drawn-out court battle that I don't remember signing it *while* I was competent."

"Ain't there something we can do?"

"Postpone the meeting."

"Get another lawyer who can do something. My cousin did some Fed time. He said there's always a loophole in the law."

"Jeanette knows what she's doing." Anger simmered in me. "I hate Hana with all my might. My pops worked hard to build our wealth. Hana didn't lay one brick, but she wants the whole building."

Sade dug between the cushions for the remote and turned the TV down. She kicked her shoes off and tucked her feet under her ass. "What if she had a car accident, a bad one?"

"I'd keep my money. Turn the TV back up."

"What I meant is...you know...we arrange the accident."

I turned to her but only my head moved. "Have you lost your mind? That's murder."

"So!" She sighed too loud. "We got away with murder before. How hard is it to do it again? You don't deserve to lose your family's shit."

"What's wrong with you?" I couldn't believe her. Not that I had given it an ounce of thought, but one body floating around in my head was enough. "We're not killers like that." *As if there was a difference.*

She twitched the corner of her mouth. "Boy, look, I'm just standing by your side. Your sister don't trust you. She think you done gone crazy. She's scared to even talk to you." Sade gestured at the house. "If you ain't satisfied with living like this, then let's do something about it. And if you're cool with this bullshit, then I ain't trying to hear no more about that white bitch and your money. Shoulda never climbed in bed with the slave master's daughter anyway." She dug a section of the daily paper from her purse and tossed it on my lap. "Taco Bell is hiring at the mall. We have to start thinking about our future." She rolled her eyes, stomped up the steps, and slammed a door.

I stood at the bottom of the steps. "I thought you were going to cook tonight."

"Fix your own damn food!" Another door slammed.

✪✪✪

I was on my way to pick up Chinese food when my cell phone rang. My ring tone sang Avant and Keke's "My First Love." Erienne. A feeling of peace consumed me as I connected the call. "Hey, lady."

"Hey, man. You're smiling."

"You have that power over me."

She said, "It sounds like you're in a car."

"Picking up dinner."

"Let me guess." She paused. "Um...it's a little after seven o'clock there, which means takeout wasn't planned. Survey says...Chinese food for one hundred."

We laughed together.

"You always said that we're connected."

"Soul mates. When something bothers you, I feel it a million miles away. I talked to my mother last night. She told me. Wanna talk about it?"

I let out a deep breath as I pulled away from a traffic light. "I tried to keep it together, but it's falling apart anyway. I can't remember doing any of the things I'm accused of."

"I'm coming home."

"You don't have to do that. I got into this mess; I'll get out of it. Where are you?"

"Flying over the Congo. My work here is done. Parrish, I love you. Love is supportive. It doesn't abandon you when you're down."

Knowing that Erienne was in my corner made all the difference in the world. "Don't come back for me. You're saving lives over there. That's the greater good."

"You're important to me, Parrish. I'm moving back home. It was planned for December, but you need me so I'm en route now. I'll be there Sunday morning."

"But your work."

"I've established an organization in the States. It's called UNITY, which is an acronym for Uniting Numbers in Today's Youth. It's still activist work; just not in the field of health care. Besides, the work here will continue; there are many dedicated to the cause." She was quiet. "I'm lonely. I'm ready for a social life; ready to start a family."

I parked in the restaurant lot. "Good thing I'm getting a divorce." I thought about Sade.

"Good thing."

"I'm seeing someone. It's complicated."

"Is your cell phone charged?"

"Yes."

"So is mine."

She didn't say one word as I explained my situation in detail.

She said, "Parrish, I love you enough to forfeit my own happiness to see you happy. I tip my hat to Sade. Pick me up at the airport. Sunday morning, okay?"

"Okay."

She hung up.

That was the problem. I had no measuring stick to determine my degree of happiness. I didn't feel that automatic magic with Sade. All I really felt was the sex. I told her that I loved her only because of our documented past. But I was really standing in the middle of the street waiting for that emotion to crash into me.

❂❂❂

A petite Asian woman handed back my credit card instead of a receipt. "Card no good." She pulled the food closer to her side of the counter, wagging a finger. "No good."

I gave her my Black Card and smiled. I watched her swipe it twice.

"This no good." She tossed it on the counter.

I looked at the five dollars in my wallet and walked out of the restaurant.

I dialed my lawyer as I settled on the car seat.

She picked up before the ring was complete. "Why haven't you returned my calls?"

"Why aren't my credit cards working?"

"If you'd return my calls, you'd know that the courts ordered all of your accounts frozen. Hana's lawyers are good. They want to finalize this."

"Can they do this?"

"If they're led to believe you're going to flee with the money. Not returning my calls and hiding out didn't make the court's decision hard."

"I literally have five dollars. Excuse my language, but what the fuck am I supposed to do with five dollars?"

"I'll loan you—"

"I can't believe this." I hung up. My stomach growled. My hatred for Hana deepened. I looked up and there was a tall guy walking in front of my car, bouncing a basketball. He reminded me of Ball Game.

Chapter 30

"One...two...three, lift," Sade said.

They dumped Ball Game's body into a laundry basket mounted on wheels. Sade covered him with their suite's linen.

"This isn't right." Parrish paced again. The idea of pushing a dead body out the back door of the hotel made him queasy. "Can't do this and live with myself."

"Damn! Why don't you chill out? It's called survival, Parrish. Self-preservation."

"I can't. I'm too nervous; you're calm like you get rid of bodies every weekend."

"Don't judge me 'cause I'm determined not to give up what we have."

"I'm not worth this type of trouble."

She touched his face and embraced him. "You're worth everything to me, more than you'll ever know." She opened the door. "Let's do this."

Strolling a dead man to the service elevator were the scariest steps Parrish had ever taken. Now he could somewhat relate to death row inmates in their final thoughts during their walk to the chamber. The only difference was that if he reached his destination, the parking lot, he would live another day with his life and freedom intact.

The elevator opened effortlessly.

"You really need to chill and get yourself together," Sade said, pressing the ground-floor button. "It's three-thirty in the morning; we'll be straight."

Sweat dripped from Parrish's chin as if his temples were leaky faucets. His drenched shirt clung to his skin. He felt a bead of water run through the crack of his ass and down his thigh. "It's hot."

"Just four more floors and we home free." She touched him as if it would comfort him.

For the next forty-eight seconds, an irritating silence bounced around the mechanical box as they watched the digital LED count down the floors to freedom.

Parrish's heart slammed itself around when the elevator opened. He felt himself shrinking as he faced a hotel employee with a nameplate that read: Dreamer.

"This is an unauthorized area," Dreamer said. "This service elevator is for staff only." She looked at them, and then at the laundry basket. "This isn't supposed to be in here, either." She grabbed the opposite side of the basket.

Parrish tugged it back toward him.

Sade stepped between Dreamer and the basket. "Girl, forgive us." She glanced at Parrish and whispered in Dreamer's ear.

Parrish watched Dreamer's face turn red. She giggled. "No wonder he's perspiring. That's kinky." She felt good from the blunt she had smoked with Ball Game.

Sade shrugged. "You gots to be creative if you wanna keep him at home."

"You're Ball Game's sister, right?"

Parrish's knees buckled. If it hadn't been for the basket he would have hit the floor. He coughed to soothe the feeling in his throat.

"Ah," Sade said, "you know m...my brother?"

"He's a hunk. I noticed his car is still in the lot. I was hoping to see him before he left. Where is he?"

Parrish said, "Asleep."

Sade tapped the basket. "That's why this thing came in handy."

"Think he'd mind if I dropped by?"

They all exchanged glances.

"What man wouldn't mind a beautiful woman coming to visit him in a hotel room in the middle of the night?" Parrish said.

They traded places.

As the elevator closed, Dreamer said, "Make sure to put the laundry cart back."

Sade punched me. "Boy, are you stupid? Why you tell her that?"

"So that she could get the hell away from us." He gave her the car keys but didn't let go of the ring.

She pulled the keys away. "Boy, I ain't gonna leave you."

"Hurry up." He took the basket to the back of the hotel and waited.

Three minutes felt like three thousand to Parrish. Please hurry. *He stared through the door. Finally Sade arrived. They scooped Ball Game in the heap of laundry and tossed him in the trunk. They combed the parking lot until Sade pointed out a BMW with a wrecked front end.*

She said, "Meet me at the house. Park his car on the street. We'll ditch it later."

"We're not separating."

"You don't know what to do with a dead man. I got this. I'm gonna dump his ass in a crack neighborhood."

"Then I'll go with you."

"Go to the house and clean yourself up. You look like you been gettin' high. They pull us over, it'll be your fault we're in jail. I got this."

As scared as he was, he would've been suspicious of himself, too. "You sure?"

"Yup." She shook her head.

"Okay." He reached for the door handle.

She stopped him to kiss him with a passion close to fire. "Go. I'll be there soon."

❀❀❀

Dreamer thought about what Sade had whispered to her and had a naughty thought as she put the key card back in her pocket. She started toward the bedroom. "Ball Game, it's Dreamer. I'm coming in, okay?" She found the room empty, the sheets missing from the bed. The bathroom was empty as well. She went to draw the curtains and saw Ball Game's car leaving the lot.

❀❀❀

I climbed in bed with Sade and was angry, hungry, and disgusted. She turned her back on me and focused on the TV. My pops had told me that when a woman turns her back on you in bed, she's pissed off.

"I—"

She threw up a hand. "I suggest you leave me the fuck alone if you don't wanna sleep downstairs."

The man on TV pointed a gun at another man's head.

My eyes widened.

She sucked her teeth and pointed the remote.

I grabbed her hand. "I want to see this."

She faced me. "But I thought this type of stuff bothers you."

"Things change." My stomach growled. "If she were to have an accident, how would we do it?"

The man pulled the trigger.

I smiled, watching the body hit the floor the same way Ball Game's had.

Sade sat up. "I got it all figured out."

"They always blame the husband."

"Not with the perfect alibi."

I studied her. "You're wicked. Should I be afraid of you?"

"Boy, please. This is about self-preservation. I'm the one who has to put up with your ass. My only interest is protecting my interest."

"Having lunch with the president is the perfect alibi."

She twitched the corner of her mouth. "Think you got the heart to commit the perfect murder?"

"If it will make everything right."

"Ever thought about what a person can get away with if everyone watching prime time news could give you an alibi?"

"I'm listening."

"In your shoes, this is how'd I'd get away with murder," she began.

Chapter 31

Sade overflowed with enthusiasm. I could see the wheels spinning in her head. "That might work." I stared at the ceiling. "The money in my safe-deposit box will cover the expenses."

"Might my ass," she said.

"Her bodyguard is the problem."

"They're *fuckin'*, Parrish. Hana won't sleep anywhere but in her bed. You ain't there. I wonder who you think will be curled up beside her."

❂❂❂

Tuesday was barefoot and naked. She limped. Each step she took fired a surge of pain through her body. Her face was smeared red with lipstick, hair tangled in a mess.

But Catherine had said it wouldn't hurt.

Catherine's gun wasn't as heavy as Tuesday had imagined. Now that she finally had her hand on it, she trembled so hard she was afraid that she would shoot too soon. She limped and pictured all the men who had climbed between her legs. Who had been too rough while playing house. Who had made her scream. *Who had soaked her with their sweat. Who had torn her.*

Her eyes glazed over and shrank to rivets. Her jawbones throbbed. The heroin and cocaine marching through her veins heightened her senses. She could smell the mattress's funk in her pores. She figured she had absorbed it into her composition.

She stood in the living room two feet from Catherine.

Catherine didn't even know Tuesday was there. Burnt matches stained the air. The dingy walls seemed like they were closing in on Tuesday. She knew that if she didn't get out, the walls would reduce her to a tiny smudge.

Catherine held a syringe between her teeth while tightening a belt around an arm. She farted and an awful stench blended with the burnt matches. Her head rolled forward when she shot the dope in her arm. Drool leaked from her mouth.

Footsteps fell behind Tuesday.

"Told you to stay in the room," she said without taking her eyes off of Catherine.

Parrish's eyes swelled with water when he saw the dark blood making tracks down Tuesday's inner thighs. "Come on, Tuesday, let's go back upstairs; get you some clothes."

"We ain't going back." She moved closer to Catherine. "She was going to let Conrad do it to you today." Tuesday raised the gun. "Said it was your time to earn money."

Catherine enjoyed the zoom. She nodded in and out of consciousness. The syringe hit the floor; she scratched a raw lesion on her neck. "Get in the bed. Don't make me go get my gun."

"Come on, Tuesday. Let's run for it right now."

All of a sudden she felt no pain. "This gun, Catherine?"

Catherine blinked twice while trying to stand.

Tuesday squeezed.

The gun jumped from her hand.

The bullet knocked Catherine back into a sitting position. She grabbed her stomach, blood wetting her fingers. "I'm... your mother."

"No, you're not!" Tuesday said, picking up the gun. "You're not."

"I don't wanna go to jail," Parrish said.

"I'm...shot." Catherine held Tuesday's gaze. "You shot me. I'm—"

"Dying." Tuesday aimed at her mother's chest this time, held on to the handle tighter, and squeezed the trigger.

✪✪✪

The Saturday morning sun shone through Tuesday's kitchen window. She adjusted her robe. "I was eleven. I looked at that white man and told him I was thinking about him and wanted him. I was already ruined. I couldn't let him violate my brother."

"That's why you won't sleep in a bed." Silence spoke his thoughts out loud.

"Why I don't wear lipstick. Why I'm scared to have kids. Why I have an arrest record for prostitution. Why I'm strung out on drugs. I'm poison; you only think you want me." She sank into a chair, avoiding his gaze. "I can't believe I told you. I've never talked about it with anyone. I'll have a plane ready by the time you get yourself together."

"I'm not leaving," Silence said, turning on the stove. "Unless you want me to."

She looked at him with disbelief. "Don't you want to?"

"No." He set a skillet on top of the flame. "You have to let it out to heal. Abuse repeats itself in secrecy. If you keep it bottled up, you'll internally abuse yourself with the same experiences. By definition, secrets are dark until you shine light on them."

"My father found out that Catherine had started getting high. He threatened to take me and my brother. Before that happened, she took us to Cleveland and changed our names, which is why my father couldn't find us." She paused and thought, enjoying the aroma consuming the kitchen. "That smells good."

"*Es huevos rancheros, y frijoles refritos con tortillas.*" He seasoned the eggs. "You reconnected with your father, that's what counts."

"Only because I found a letter he had written to Catherine. When Parrish and I went to the return address, it was our grandmother's. Last Catherine knew, my father was a clerk at a gas station. Had she known that he was making money in the film business, I'm sure she would have ransomed us. I wouldn't be ruined now."

"There's nothing wrong with you. How you're responding to your past is the problem."

The phone rang and Tuesday excused herself. Silence cooked breakfast and thought about what he could do to cause her to smile.

She came back into the kitchen in worse condition than she had left.

"I take it that wasn't a good call." He eased the refried beans from a pot onto their plates.

"For once in my life I'm enjoying myself. I have to go back to Jersey, and I don't want to."

"It's your brother again?"

"That was Hana. She wants to make a deal with me to drop the charges against Parrish, keep him running the company, and leave him with fifty percent of his net worth."

"That's positive." He sat down in front of his plate. "She could play hardball with her leverage."

"She's greedy, so her offering to be generous rubs me wrong. I've never trusted her. She wants to meet with me next Saturday. Go with me. I can only tolerate so much of Hana. It would mean a lot to me if you were there when I come up for air."

"Whatever came of your mother? Did she ever get it together?"

"You mean Catherine."

He nodded.

She remembered the look on Catherine's face when the last bullet had torn into her. Tuesday pulled in a breath. "Heard she overdosed."

✪✪✪

I was taking my medicine and watching CNN when the phone on the nightstand rang. "Hello."

"Boy, I thought your bitch and Doctor Rodriguez didn't know each other." Sade spoke lower than normal.

"From my understanding, they don't." I thought back to a conversation I had had with Hana about my not allowing her to meet my doctor or become involved with my counseling. "As a matter of fact, they don't. Why? And why are you whispering? Speak up."

"I can't; they'll hear me eavesdropping on their conversation. Hana is in Doctor Rodriguez's office now; I'm listening to them over the intercom."

"What business does Hana have there?" At this point, I hated to speak her name. It tasted like shit in my mouth. The sound of it reinforced my desire to do her bodily harm.

"If I knew what they was doing, I wouldn't hafta be eavesdropping on their conversation. I'll tell you this, though," she said matter-of-factly, "they ain't strangers. Uh-uh. Not talking 'bout how long each other's hair has grown."

Sade's words trickled through my thoughts. Why would Hana lie to me about her acquaintance with Doctor Rodriguez? I flipped that around a few more times and came to the conclusion that Sade either misunderstood what she thought she'd heard, or she just flat out didn't know what the hell she was talking about. It made no logical sense for Hana to have lied. "There's nothing to it. Doctor Rodriguez knows about me and you. Obviously there's nothing to be suspicious of because they would've never met there, knowing you'd bring it back to me."

"Same thing I thought. We can rule that out because they don't know I'm here."

"You're on the clock."

"Out of the blue, Rodriguez gives me the day off. Said something urgent came up and that she was canceling all her appointments." She said that like she was pissed with me for insinuating the need of an explanation. "I forgot my keys and doubled back. I saw that big guy leaving the office. You know, the one you said you remember from somewhere. When I came in, I heard them running they mouths."

My mind relaxed some. "You didn't actually see Hana?" That was not a question.

"No, but you know how nosey I am. I turned on the intercom and got an earful. They was talking 'bout some stupid book... ah... Push...something or the other."

"*Push Comes To Shove*," I almost hated to say.

"Yup, that's it. Hana was bragging that she was co-starring in the movie version. It's bad, Parrish."

"Who are you telling?"

"I mean it gets worse."

I seriously doubted that. "Impossible."

"Hana told the doc that once your estate was legally

hers, she would pay the doc her portion as planned. I started to bust up in there and beat both them heifers down, but I called you first. Just give me the word and them hoes' asses are as good as kicked."

"That is such a quixotic story. Don't insult my intelligence with your lies."

"I don't even know what the hell that word means. But you know what...kiss my black ass. I ain't got no reason to lie. What the fuck for? You ate my pussy last night, not Hana's. Your ashy, crusty ass is curled up in my sex-stained sheets right now, not Hana's. What's the fuckin' point of lying when I'm winning? Boy, I'm on your motherfuckin' side! It'll do you good to remember it." She sighed much too loudly. "Get something to write with."

"Whatever it is just tell me," I said, feeling small. "And I am not ashy."

"Yeah, you'd like to think so. Write the info down."

I fumbled through the nightstand for a pen and paper. "What am I writing?"

"They going to lunch. I'm giving you the address of the restaurant. See for your damn self."

Ten minutes after Sade hung up on me, I was on my way out the door when the bell rang. I pulled open the door. A paunchy black man handed me an envelope and said, "We'll be in touch, Mr. Clovis." He trotted down the sidewalk.

The four pictures I removed from the envelope, taken

at the New York School of Performing Arts, caused my skin to crawl. There was a note that read: *ten million dollars for the answers to the questions you have.*

✪✪✪

The paunchy man climbed into Jeanette's car and fanned the cigar smoke.

"Does he have the envelope?"

The man nodded.

Chapter 32

Anger seeped through Jeanette's pores. She scowled at the other women. She spoke around a smoldering cigar, "We agreed to never meet in public." She smacked a hand on the restaurant table, which caused the silverware and dishes to squeal. "This is reckless! You're jeopardizing years of planning. Had I any way of knowing that you'd even dream of pulling a stunt like this, I would've never chosen you to work Parrish."

"Excuse me, ladies," a frail man—who was thin to the point of approaching anorexia—said. "This is a non-smoking establishment. You'll have to put that out."

Jeanette squared her shoulders. She drew hard on the cigar. "It'll be out when I'm done."

"Ma'am—"

"Hey! Get your fucking foot off my nerve." She dunked the cigar in a pitcher of water. She jabbed her finger at the other women. "Neither one of you...I swear he better not get a tip."

Hana and Doctor Rodriguez laughed as the man slithered away.

"There's no reason to blow this," Jeanette said. "We

got ourselves a sure thing. You're the abused wife that everyone loves. Lucinda, you have the medical aspect of this con covered. The media is eating this up. Who doesn't know that Parrish is Waco, Texas? Today isn't payday, so why in the fuck am I here?"

Hana raised her glass. "The best actresses are those who improvise well."

"I'll toast to that." Lucinda raised her glass, too.

✪✪✪

Shamar sat at the bar watching the girls while speaking into a cell phone: "This time next week, we'll be very rich men."

"Not many men marry their childhood sweethearts on Saturday, knowing that they'll be widowers the following Sunday," Ball Game said.

"With the money Hana's gonna leave us, I can buy a new sweetheart."

"There are still other hungry mouths."

Shamar glanced at Lucinda and Jeanette. "They'll die of starvation once I have the money. I'll call you when it's time."

✪✪✪

Lucinda emptied her glass and traced the rim. "I don't trust Shamar."

Hana considered him while flashing a smile. "His usefulness has reached its expiration date. We're dividing this pie by five, ladies. He won't live long enough to even taste it."

"I never could stand his ass," Jeanette said, waving at him.

"The pictures." Lucinda rested her elbows on the table. She leaned in. "It's important that he has them or this gathering is—"

"I took care of it," Jeanette said.

✪✪✪

I was numb. I couldn't feel the steering wheel trapped between my fists. I didn't want to try to make sense of this. The only thing I wanted was for Sade to shake me awake. I wanted her to stop me from having this nightmare. I watched them through the restaurant window from my car. It angered me to see their lips moving without knowing the content of their conversation.

It ached me.

I turned my attention to the picture on my lap, the four devils in it, the date on which it had been taken: 1996. More important, I paid close attention to what the picture did and didn't reveal. When I refocused back on my wife, my lawyer, and my doctor, I knew that they were in my life to steal quarters.

I crumpled the picture and drove away. At first I had

agreed to kill Hana based on self-preservation. But now... now...I was going to murder her because it would make me feel better.

✪✪✪

At 7:35 Sunday morning, I drove Sade to work because her car had a flat tire.

"You been actin' all stank since yesterday," she said.

I could feel her eyes on me. "It's bothering me that I can't figure out what Hana and Doctor Rodriguez were doing together." I never told her that Jeanette was there also. I'm not sure why I hadn't.

"Irregardless, you making me uncomfortable. Is you takin' your medicine?"

"Stop reminding me that I have issues. I can't pick up the newspaper or turn on the TV without being reminded. I don't need it from you as well."

"Excuse me for worrying about your tired ass."

I eased the car under the awning of her office building. "See you later."

"So, it's like that?" She sucked her teeth and folded her arms like a spoiled brat. "No kiss, a have-a-nice-day, a fuck you, or nothing?"

I pecked her on the mouth.

She rolled her eyes. "I ain't tryin' to be worried 'bout you all day. Call me." She leaned over to rub my thigh. "I know you hurting, Parrish; I wish I could take it all away. I'm down with you."

Get out first came to mind. I was on a mission; she was slowing down my progress. "I'll call."

❂❂❂

By 9:45 AM. I was on my way back to Sade's with Erienne. I had told her everything I knew...and what I thought I knew.

She sighed, looking at me as if the information were too much to process. She didn't say a word while she studied me. She was beautiful to the point it made me bashful. Her skin was the color of toast and glowed like honey; her locks flowed past her shoulders; and her dimples amplified her being. When she had exited the plane, I was instantly mesmerized by her body. Nine years ago, I had witnessed a skinny young adult board an Africa-bound flight. Today, the woman who came back to me was curvy and well developed in all the right places. Even while sitting on the passenger's seat her hips made a bold statement.

When she finally spoke, it was all business. She said, "I'm in-terested in knowing what you remember doing a couple of hours before each blackout."

"The first time—"

"Let's start from the night that Hana was raped."

I hated to revisit that night. "She and I were stuck in traffic. We had a disagreement concerning our sexual... It was pretty nasty. A while later I was in bed thinking about the events that led to us arguing. Hana came in with wine, with the intentions of having makeup sex. We had a glass of wine and..."

"Sex."

I nodded. "I awoke, maybe an hour later, with these angry cops standing over me."

"The other times, did you have anything to eat or drink before you blacked out?"

"I can't remember."

"It's important that you try."

"Think so." I shrugged. "I don't remember exactly what I had. But it was nothing outside of my ordinary eating and drinking habits."

"Now what I need for you to remember is whether you fed yourself, or did someone else feed you?" She watched me while I thought.

And I thought.

And thought some more. "Hana."

"Turn left here." Erienne pointed at a four-way intersection. "I have a friend at the University of Medicine and Dentistry."

"Is it important that you see her now?" I made the left.

"I don't recall saying my friend was a her." Now she smiled.

"I apologize."

"No need. You'll enjoy Tasia. This visit isn't about me. It's about you."

"No offense, but I've had it with doctors."

"You need a toxicology test. I want to know if there's anything foreign in your bloodstream. Nothing you've told me sits well; I'm going to get to the bottom of it to satisfy myself."

I gave her my cell phone. "Think you can get Tuesday down here? She won't accept or return my calls."

"She's scared of you." Erienne shook her head with a smirk on her face. "I suppose she's still ducking problems there aren't simple solutions to."

"I thought I was the only one who knew her."

"Is she still using drugs as a means of escape?"

"Old habits are hard to break."

Chapter 33

It was the smell of alcohol that first registered when Tuesday opened the door. Then her desire to taste it followed.

"Let's party." A quasi-attractive Filipina with distinctive facial features barged in the house. "I scored us an ounce of Colombian coke; I'm dying to try it."

"Song, you're drunk." Tuesday led her to the sofa.

"Only a notch past tipsy." She waved a package of white powder in a teasing manner. "Undress. I can't wait to lick this candy from your poonani."

❂❂❂

Silence stopped in midstride. He adjusted a towel around his waist and watched Tuesday and Song from the darkness of the hall adjacent to the living room.

❂❂❂

Tuesday's mouth watered. She honed in on the cocaine that was swaying in Song's hand. Her stomach churned;

her skin prickled with goose bumps; and her body dampened with a chilled sweat. She gnashed her teeth while anticipating the high. A week ago, Tuesday would have stripped naked before she could have bolted the door. Her focus narrowed on Song's hand. *A little taste wouldn't hurt.*

"Come on, girl," Song's words dragged. "Turn some music on and show me some skin. I'm your friend. You shouldn't make me wait so long. I come straight to you when I score."

A quiet settled in as the women held gazes. Tuesday heard Silence's shower water running. She held her breath to stop her nerves from dancing. *Move forward, you've been here too long.* "Song, get up."

"I wanna do it to you right here." She patted the sofa. "No floor today."

"We're not doing anything." Tuesday guided her to the door. "You have to leave."

"I have the coke, but you have the nerve to have an attitude. That's not an admirable way to treat your friend."

"We ain't friends, Song. A real friend wouldn't try to get me high or manipulate me for sex." Tuesday sucked in a breath. "I'm done, washing my hands."

"You're no better than me: a bottom-of-the-barrel addict with money." Song's tone was splashed with derision. "You're not fooling nobody but yourself. When you come to the little senses you have left, call me. I'll treat you to a bag and a great fuck."

"Good luck." Tuesday shut the door on Song and, hopefully, substance abuse. "I wish us both the best."

Silence smiled. He decided that what he wanted to give her could wait until after his shower.

✪✪✪

Tuesday's nerves were still unbalanced, but one thing was certain: She felt stronger than ever. She knew that there was a long road ahead of her. A road that she'd never had the courage to look at, much less travel. She was uncertain of where it would lead, but she was no longer afraid to discover the unknown.

The phone rang for the sixth time.

"Hello," Tuesday said.

"You sound down."

"Actually, it's the opposite. Who am I speaking with?"

"Erienne."

"Girl, I haven't heard from you in...almost...forever. How are you? What's going on with you?"

"To be honest, I'll be fine when I get clarity on Parrish's dilemma."

Tuesday thought back to when Parrish had called her from jail. "I swear I didn't believe it when I got the call. Not even after I saw Hana. It had to be a dream. Parrish wouldn't even fight in school. The only thing he ever showed disfavor to was men abusing women. I refused to believe that he was capable of doing something like that to her." She began to feel like the dirty breakfast dishes scattered about the kitchen. "Despite Parrish's brief bouts with psychiatrists over the years, I never really thought he had serious mental issues. I thought he was dealing with our mother on his own terms." She filled the sink with soapy water. "He did it, Erienne. He hurt her. I don't know who the last person was I saw that looked like Parrish, but I assure you, he wasn't my brother."

Erienne stole a furtive look at Parrish as he navigated them toward the hospital. She studied him for signs of disturbance for the third time in twenty minutes. "I'm confident now that I'm with him. We're going to the hospital."

Tuesday's heartbeat quickened. "I'm balancing on a frayed thread right now; I can't handle any more bad news."

"Everything's fine. However, something strange is happening. We all need to put our heads together and figure it out."

"I'm meeting with Hana this coming Saturday. I can't say I'll be ready to see Parrish or whoever he may be on that day."

"There are some pictures you need to see today. It's a dirty game being played, and your lawyer has something to do with it."

"Parrish is going too damn far now. He has to accept the consequences of his actions. How dare he lead you to believe Jeanette is involved in anything?"

"We'll narrow it down when you get here. Right or wrong, Parrish needs you. Your jet is in Malibu waiting."

Silence strolled up and caressed Tuesday's shoulders from behind. He could feel the tension bottled inside her.

Tuesday lost herself in his touch. She nibbled on her lip, and said, "I'll be there." She ended the call and stared at the dirty dishes, wondering if it would be as easy to clean up her life as it would be to clean up the dishes.

Silence handed her a folded piece of paper. "I believe in you."

She saw the truth resonating in his eyes. "I really needed to hear you say that." She studied the paper. "What is it?"

"Just a little something I wrote for you."

She unfolded the paper.

Secrets

Some secrets are not destined to suffocate inside damp
   dungeons of closed mouths.
Echoing pains and scars stained on flesh are the shading
   on canvases that make art...breathe.
Faded maps and shattered footprints still hold direction.
Don't hide the true North of you from sailors seeking
   the shore of your presence.
Find your chains, mold me into that key, unlock
   your wings.
You belong to the sky's freedom...
Where your hidden diary entries can fatten clouds with
   rain that will cascade and scrub the air clean.

I've seen your tears quench parched lips—soak into mine.

You are words on blank pages.

Let me trace my fingers over the paragraphs of you—your unwritten story.

Harsh histories can chisel elegant sculptures from naked marble that lead questions to remember that they too are answers.

Don't hide the sanctuary of you from the world.

At first, darkness fears the candlelight and retreats into "safe" corners.

As the flame gently drinks in the dark, it surrenders to the illumination of its light.

"Safe" corners are prisons for messengers of the light you shine.

I know careless touches can harden hearts to stone.

But water passionately dripping on the surface of a stone will carve a fluid stream through its center.

Swim with me.

Reverberate within a loving embrace not seeking to clip your wings. It does exist.

Even though it hurts at times...you teach through you. By continuing to exist, you love the world without knowing it.

Know it!

Even birth hurts as it ushers in new life.

Go into labor, and let me be the ears that the secret of you is revealed to.

Chapter 34

A few ticks past three o'clock we were gathered in Sade's living room. The curtains were drawn. The room was dim. I stood near the mantelpiece while the pictures changed hands.

Tuesday's jawbones throbbed. "I'm thoroughly pissed." She passed the pictures to Silence—not that he knew who he was looking at.

"This is about money." I paced. "They're in for a rude awakening because I'm putting a stop to it."

"We're going to help you end it," Erienne said. "There's a high content of Rohypnol present in his toxicology screen, which explains the loss of time and blackouts. Rohypnol hasn't been prescribed to him. Someone is drugging him."

"I know I'm an outsider here," Silence said, "but...it doesn't make a lot of sense to me. These people—" He motioned to the pictures. "—are going through a lot of trouble to give you a date-rape drug just to make you think you're crazy. If this is all about money, there are much easier ways to get it." He dismissed the pictures. "From my understanding, you are taking medicine, aren't you?"

"Something I considered as well." Erienne went to her purse, gave Tuesday my prescription bottle, and then returned to her seat. "Take one. Matter of fact, take them all."

My thoughts drifted to an unpleasant place. Shooting Hana was too...humane. A slow death over many days of excruciating pain would prove justifiable.

Tuesday studied the pill bottle. Her features grim, eyebrows bunched. "Why would I take these?"

"Because it's a placebo," I said. "Powdered sugar."

"Not one drop of Lithium Carbonate in his system." Erienne licked her lips. "Apparently, Hana thought it was worth it to stage all of this."

All of a sudden I heard, "Catch!"

Tuesday threw the pill bottle.

I watched it flipping end over end. I snatched it from the air with a perfect overhand catch.

Then everything changed.

Tuesday seemed to shrink. The more she withdrew, the more her fleeting energy sucked life out of the room. Silence was on his feet, standing guard.

She stood behind Silence, clearly terrified. She talked over his shoulder. Her words were slow, confident, and precise. "Erienne, get your shit. We're getting the hell out of here." She paused for effect. "This ain't Parrish. His doctor told me how to identify his primary personality from the alter. We're being manipulated."

I said, "Tuesday, you've got to be kidding me. Doctor Rodriguez is in on this. You see the pictures."

Silence clenched his fists, warning me that he was prepared to thump for his love interest. "I don't believe you, either. For all we know you could've put these people in this picture. Looks like the work of Photoshop to me."

Erienne was standing beside me now. "Everyone needs to relax. There's no reason to be at odds with one another."

"No!" Tuesday said. "You need to wisen up and use your head." She kept her eyes boring into me. "Parrish has been diagnosed with schizophrenia, thanks to Catherine screwing him up. It's been proven that the best doctors misdiagnose personality disorders for schizophrenia, right?"

I literally watched Tuesday's fright increase. It communicated itself through her body language. She was trembling. The last time I'd seen her this afraid, I was locked in a closet watching her being molested through a keyhole.

Silence was ready to attack.

"Answer me."

"Yes," Erienne said, nodding. She said it like the realization pained her. "In a high percentage of cases, the patient travels his entire medical journey diagnosed with schizophrenia. It's not discovered that the actual problem is an identity disorder until the patient is an adult."

"Glad you figured it out." Tuesday took hold of Silence's hand. "We're out of here. He raped Hana. All this bullshit is to make us think he's the victim. His alter is smart like that. If you have as much common sense as I think you have, you'd be leaving with us."

"Tuesday!" I called behind her but she never broke stride. "You promised to always protect me." The words caused her to stagger.

She looked over her shoulder and locked eyes with me. "It's me."

She broke our connection and kept going.

"Wait a minute, please," Erienne said. "What makes you so sure that this is his alter?"

"My brother is right-handed." Now she burned me with contemptuous eyes. "This guy caught the pills with his left. There was no reason to when I was sitting directly across from where he was standing. His alter favors the left." She led Silence through the front door.

Erienne backed away from me. I felt her energy go cold and change the atmosphere of the living room. She zoomed in on the pills in my left hand. "I've never known you to be left-handed, either."

"I'm not one or the other; I'm even handed: ambidextrous." I took in a breath, wondering if I should try explaining at the risk of pushing her away. I figured the truth was best: "I awoke one morning in a homeless shelter with my right hand injured. As a result of nursing my right hand back healthy, I started using my left more frequently."

She was quiet, obviously thinking. She broke the quiet and said, "As many times as you've touched me, made love to me, I would know that you're efficient with both hands. I distinctly remember you being right-handed."

I moved toward her.

"Don't."

"Come on, Erienne, you know—"

"Stay away from me, Parrish." Her words were deliberate and sharp. "You're scaring me." She went to the door quicker than Tuesday had. "The placebo, the pictures, the Rohypnol in your system, the conspiracy against your money; it can all be an attempt to manipulate me like Tuesday said."

I began to erode knowing that the two people I cared most about in this world didn't trust me. "Use your head, Erienne."

"I am." She slammed the door behind her.

❂❂❂

Outside in the car, Silence touched Tuesday's hand. "You can cry now; I'll hold you close."

She buried her head in his chest and unraveled. "I can't help him right now." Her tears spotted Silence's shirt. "I need help right now. I need the strength to concentrate on plugging the holes in my raggedy life."

He rubbed her back in small, soothing circles. "You're all that counts. Parrish will work through his problems. He has no choice in the matter. That's how life unfolds. Our experiences, good and seemingly bad ones, give us the opportunity to deepen our understanding of ourselves, and they show us where we are spiritually."

"It's all happening at once: you, my brother, my addiction are all tugging on me. Too much is unfolding."

"The more you struggled with today, the more you'll love and appreciate tomorrow." He tapped the horn when Erienne strolled by crying.

❉❉❉

Within minutes I had arrived at a place I'd been ducking my entire life—alone. I loosened my shirt collar because the isolation was on the verge of strangling me to death. After several deep breaths and many attempts to wet my dry lips, I thought about the faces in the pictures. But what I wanted more than anything at this moment was to know who was responsible for delivering them to me. I thumbed through the envelope and noticed a picture was missing. I had another thought and dialed the number of the only person who hadn't yet turned on me.

"Upscale Pictures. Andrea speaking."

"Were you able to get the information?"

"Yes, well...as much as I could." I heard her shuffle through some papers. "All of the vacations took place during a period of seven months. The same seven months I was out on maternity leave."

"Meahgan," I said. "She was the girl who filled in for you."

"Correct. Meahgan Broadwater. She worked for Paid Today Temporary Agency, according to our records."

"Give me the number and address. I need to talk to this woman."

"She's dead, Mr. Clovis. Her body washed up in the Hudson with multiple gunshots. But get this: they found her the same day you were arrested for…you know. But the company doesn't exist. There is no listing in the directories and nothing comes up on Google, nothing other than news of Meahgan's murder. If Google can't find the company, it's a ghost."

I weighed what she had said along with everything else I'd learned. It disturbed me. "Thank you, Andrea. Did you secure media coverage for Saturday?"

"All the major networks and their affiliates will be there. Mr. Parrish?"

"Yes."

"Whatever it is you're up to, be careful."

"I'll try." I set the phone down beside me and stared at the man in the picture with a cigarette dangling from his lips. *Where do I know you from?* I sat back against the chair, gripped its arms, and thought about it real hard.

Chapter 35

Shamar's knee started to ache, a constant annoyance. He willed the pain away and checked his watch: 10:59 PM. He knew Hana and Parrish were scheduled to be home within the next hour. Then, he would execute the first part of the plan. He puffed on a Winston while focusing on a portrait of them smiling on a sandy beach with an ocean backdrop.

He admired their immense home peppered with antiquated furnishing and expensive amenities. Very soon he would be wealthy enough to own several gargantuan homes like this one. In fact, this one would become a part of his collection once everything unfolded. He puffed the cigarette many times more and wondered what Hana and Parrish were thinking about at the moment the picture had been taken. It didn't matter, he concluded. He checked his watch again: 11:03 PM. Won't be long now. *He made his way to the library.*

He approached Rudy, who was proudly standing on his perch in the center of the library. "Dumb bird. I bet you just eat and shit, don't you?" *He reached out with the intent of stroking Rudy's inviting feathers.* "Can you talk?"

Rudy locked on Shamar's finger, applying enough pressure to taste blood, to let Shamar know that he could easily dish out much more.

"Ow!" Shamar winced, snatching his hand away. "You rotten motherfucker. Do that shit again." He sucked the red goo from his finger and stepped back. He whipped his cell phone out and pressed the speed-dial feature.

The phone rang.

Rudy watched.

"Yeah," Ball Game said after the third ring.

"It's started."

"Good."

"Won't be long now." Shamar frowned at Rudy.

"Awk, suck my dick," Rudy said, to Shamar's disbelief.

Shamar was right: It wouldn't be much longer now. Not at all. He went to the wine cellar to wait as instructed. All the while he nursed his finger. He was having trouble willing that pain away.

❂❂❂

Parrish jabbed in the access code at the entrance of his home. He turned to Hana, punctuating his words with the same finger he'd jabbed the keypad with. "While I'm your husband, don't you ever let me hear you speak about having sex with other men. I better not even feel like you were thinking about that. Or, I swear, I'll do something that I may one day regret. You're going to respect me and this marriage." His voice was raised in order to speak over their neighbor's noisy Rottweiler. He noticed a marble statue standing erect near their shrubbery. "When did you buy that?"

She followed his gaze. "I didn't. You had it delivered two days ago. Said it was a gift for me." Her voice had the tone of genuine concern when she said, "You assured me that you had things under control. Can't you remember—"

"I'm okay." He ran his hands over his head. Not being able to remember things embarrassed the hell out of him. "For God's sake, would you shut up!" he yelled at the dog.

"Dogs bark, Parrish."

"If I had my way, I'd put an end to that dog's racket."

When they were on the inside of the house, he froze in his tracks. "You smell that?"

"No," she said as her heels clicked across the floor.

"Smells like someone has been smoking a cigarette in here."

"I don't smell anything." She decided that now was the perfect time to make up. She knew that a bottle of wine would do the trick.

❊❊❊

Parrish lay in bed uncomfortably. He tried hard not to think of his wife or his sister—an internal goal that failed him. Tuesday had abruptly ended their call minutes ago. He, however, still held the phone in his hand. Nothing had gone right tonight. He was angry with himself for not handling that fantasy disagreement better, more tactfully. Yet his anger toward Hana was of equal measures. He had grown beyond the point of being sickened of his marriage oscillating between existing states of make-believe, happiness, and uncertainty.

At that moment he thought of Erienne; and, for the first time in over an hour, he found himself smiling. He knew that had he and Erienne married, life would be a constant smile. She added color to his world.

The phone, locked in his fist, started shouting.

The elevator door, opposite the bed, slid open.

His smile dissolved.

Hana stepped out looking exactly like the hooker he had pictured in his mind when he'd learned of her fantasy. The camisole and thong she wore, he once thought of it as sexy. Now, one word came to mind: trashy. She had a bottle of Monticello Sangiovese and two wineglasses.

"Stinkin' slut," Rudy said from the nightstand.

Parrish often wondered if, somehow, Rudy were capable of speaking his private thoughts, if they were intuitively connected.

Hana strutted over to the wet bar. "Make up with me... please."

"There's an image in my head that I'm not appreciative—"

"Don't talk, Parris, just fuck me." She was fully aware that her dirty mouth would get his attention. She never spoke that way. "Anything that doesn't suit you, deal with the issue in bed. I'll be more cooperative." She pranced around, making sure he got a good look at her bare essentials. She prepared a special drink and then gave it to him.

"Awk, don't trust the bitch," Rudy said, walking the length of the nightstand.

"I'm going to glue your beak shut." She moved toward the bed; her eyes on Rudy. "You're the devil." She gave Parrish

the drink. "Wet your whistle. The passion you're about to en-counter, you'll need a drink."

"Thank you." He couldn't put a finger on the cause of Hana's behavior. Maybe it had something to do with the full moon, or perhaps it was the make-believe part of their rela-tionship.

She gulped down a second drink and then dropped the glass. "Goodness gracious, there's a fire blazing deep inside of me that hungers for extinguishing."

Rudy looked as if he wished he would have learned other foul words. The barking of their neighbor's dog floated in through the window. Parrish avoided Rudy's gaze. He didn't understand what was driving Hana but figured he might as well enjoy the ride.

He set the empty glass down. "Where's the fire, ma'am?"

"In here, Mr. Fireman." She buried her hand inside of the thong. "Right here."

✪✪✪

Shamar's watch alarm ruptured the deafening quiet of the wine cellar. He made his move.

✪✪✪

A bulge formed beneath the sheet around Parrish's groin. "A fire in a place like that can get out of hand if it's not taken care of. To get that nasty thing under control, the first thing

I'll need to do is get past these." He hooked her underwear with a finger.

She scooted the thong down her legs, causing him to unconsciously hold his breath. "That should accommodate." She eased the sheet back and found his erection poking through the vent of his boxer shorts. She caressed his penis long enough to raise his breathing, then she mounted him.

Parrish loved the sound she made when he pushed into her. He was obsessed with it.

"Put my fire out. It's so hot for you, Mr. Fireman."

They kissed in sync with their winding bodies. She sat upright, rocking her groin against his as if she were under a spell. The bed began to squeak. He had promised her a thousand times that he would tighten the frame. One more day wouldn't hurt. He closed his eyes. He was consumed by the moment.

The elevator doors opened.

Parrish's motor skills malfunctioned. His mind raced in fifth gear, replaying a million discussions at once. One crept by in slow motion: Hana's wanting to have sex with two men. He was sluggish but his anger staggered back.

Hana unzipped Shamar's pants, never breaking stride with Parrish.

In Parrish's world everything faded to black. Visions of his wife with another man pounded against his thoughts as hard as Hana was pounding against his groin.

He opened his eyes. He imagined the vision that played in his head: Hana having oral sex with a stranger.

Rudy watched. "Awk, stinkin' slut."

Parrish clamped his eyes tight this time, determined to force the image out, easing into oblivion.

Shamar held Hana's head between his palms while an orgasm ripped through him. "That...that felt good! I miss you, slim. I can't wait to take this bastard's money and be done with it." He buttoned his pants and looked down on Parrish with something close to pity. "Sucker."

Hana stepped into her thong. "How long will he be out?"

"I only gave him a roofie strong enough to keep him under for fifteen, twenty minutes tops." He pushed his rough hands inside a pair of leather gloves and lit a Winston.

She looked at his gloved hands and had second thoughts. She had witnessed Shamar beat a man within inches of his life. The only reason the man didn't die was Shamar wanted it that way.

He knew her well enough to understand the language of her body. "You and Jeanette came up with this plan. It's just an unofficial acting job with a heavy paycheck. For thirty-two million, I'll dig up my grandmother and knock the hell out of her." He wasn't joking in the slightest. "Now, let's get it over with. I'm tired of waking up without you."

She sat on the edge of the bed beside Parrish, watching his chest rise and fall. She turned her focus on Shamar, who was thinking of nothing other than spending Parrish and Tuesday's fortune.

"Okay," she said. A tear fell onto her breast. "Don't get carried away. I will begin filming Push Comes To Shove *soon."*

He traced the contour of her lips. His touch was gentle. The way he had always been toward her from the moment of their first touch in acting school. Acting was a hobby he felt compelled to take up after the service while he worked as a police officer in Hoboken. He caressed her face, contemplating her beauty. "It has to look good." He stroked her hair and then clenched a knot of it in a fist. "You should close your eyes." The cigarette smoldered in the corner of his mouth. After watching several tears leak from behind her lids, he proceeded to ram a fist into her face, with total disregard of her request for leniency.

She wailed and writhed in agony. Her head jerked directionless under the weight of his blows. Her tears mixed with a bloody nose and slobber. The assault lasted seventeen seconds over a minute. When Shamar finished strategically battering her body with punches, he put an ammonia capsule beneath her nose.

Her eyes fluttered open as she found consciousness.

"You did well, slim. I'm proud of you." He kissed her busted lip and then licked her blood from his own. Suddenly, he punched Parrish in the jaw, balled the unconscious man's left hand into a fist and banged it against the headboard. "That's for getting too comfortable with my woman."

He stepped onto the elevator. "Handle our business. I'll set the alarm on my way out."

Hana's body ached. She plucked the phone from Parrish's nightstand and dialed a three-digit number.

"Nine-one-one, what is your emergency?"

Hana screamed, and then said, "It was my husband...he... he raped me." She could still smell Shamar's cigarette.

And Rudy continued to watch. "Stinkin' slut."

Chapter 36

On Monday morning, Parrish awoke drenched. He popped up like a jack-in-the-box, causing Sade to stir forty-five minutes prematurely. He scrambled through the hall and down the narrow staircase, bumping into walls on his way. He sat in front of an envelope and tried to swallow, but the lump in his throat was too thick. Knowing that his dream had guided him here, he dumped the pictures out and scattered them about the table. On first sight of the man with a cigarette pinched between his lips, Parrish dropped a fist on the table. He remembered the first time he'd laid eyes on Shamar. It had been in his bedroom, the night he was accused of assault and rape.

He collected his car keys from the kitchen, tightened the belt of his housecoat, and then left the house.

❁❁❁

Detective Duval Michaels considered the pictures once more, and then glared at Parrish across a wobbly desk. "That is the most outrageous bullshit I've ever heard. Shamar Lindsay? Shamar was one of the best damn cops

I've ever had the privilege of punching the clock with."

"It's true," I said. "I'm not crazy."

"You dress well for a man who has it all together. I arrested you that night; I saw the bruises on your hand and what you did to your wife. You've been arrested for indecent exposure since then. Your mental health has been discussed in the news all month. Now you walk in my office, wearing a fuckin' striped robe and dress shoes, shooting an oral enema up my ass."

"Are you playing detective, or are you the real deal, Mr. Duval?" I scooted the chair back and stood to leave. "As eager as you were to hurt me that night, under manufactured allegations, I would have never thought you'd display apathy toward the opportunity to put the real criminals behind bars. Maybe I should learn to lower my expectations of those who enforce the law." I opened the door, thinking. I should have slowed down and dressed properly. "My pops once told me that you can never measure the content and character of a man by his clothes. If there were a possibility that I was telling the truth, I wonder what a real detective would do."

✪✪✪

Five days later, the radio played in the background of Silence's small apartment. Shakira sang about the sounds of her body and how her hips didn't lie as he watched Tuesday sleep. This was the first time she had slept in a bed since she was a child. She seemed to be at peace with her face pressed against the pillow. He hated to bother her but he had to. He shook her until she stirred and stretched.

He admired her for a while, and then said, "Hey, you." He'd grown accustomed to being in her presence, sharing the same space, breathing the same air.

"Umm, your bed... God, it's so comfortable." She blinked the remnants of sleep away. "I can't remember the last time I rested so well."

"I said the same thing when I got out of prison. Those bunks in the joint will break you up something fierce."

"What time is it?"

"Almost noon," he said as he drew the curtains, letting the sunlight overrun the room. He returned to the bed and sat beside her. "I was wrong; you need to see this." He gave her the picture. "How many people are in this picture?"

She plucked the picture from his hand and half-looked at it. "Four."

He pulled a magnifying glass from his pocket. "Now take a look. Check out the school's window. Photoshop didn't create this. Whoever took it, their reflection is in the window."

She almost choked when she saw the person in the reflection.

"So you do know her?"

She threw the covers back. "Where's the phone?"

"I don't have a land line. I tried calling my probation officer this morning but both our cell phones need charging. What's up?"

Tuesday started plucking her clothes from the floor in a hurry. "I have to talk to my brother."

✪✪✪

Sade and I stood on the stairs of Upscale's Learjet. We were overlooking a large crowd of over-caffeinated reporters. Minicams with the initials ABC, CBS, CNN, and NBC splattered on them were focused on us. Andrea had arranged for them all to be here; some of their network affiliates had even shown up.

Boom microphones dangled about our heads. Brilliant bursts of light exploded from cameras every few seconds. Minus some details, my immediate surroundings put me in the frame of mind of an outdoor movie set.

I waved the antsy reporters and camera persons quiet. "As my representative has indicated, our few moments together are to be aired live. No takeouts. You may begin recording."

Sade eased an arm around my waist. We watched several tally lights come alive on the minicams, a clear indication that a live feed was being broadcasted.

"Did you gather us here to publicly confess to assaulting and raping your wife, Mr. Clovis?" That was the same flabby Korean woman with varicose veins who'd pushed my buttons outside of the county jail.

I held on to Sade's tiny hand. "This press conference is about a confession." I could hear the blustery wind behind me, sweeping down the tarmac. "I love my wife; it was never my deliberate intention to hurt her or to expose her to danger."

"So, you're admitting to the allegations made against you?" someone said.

Now that is a decent person, I thought. He didn't come across as prying and accusatory. His tone proved that he hadn't already convicted me like the majority had. I appreciated the fact that he had made it a point of stating that the issue was only an allegation; that his snooping and probing wasn't done with carelessness.

"I take full responsibility for what happened to Hana. All last month I heard various news sources—most of whom are present today—misinform the public about my state of mental affairs. This was an issue that I never wanted probed or opened to public speculation. I was ashamed of it. All my life I wanted to be normal. I was abused as a child; as a result, I developed schizophrenia, which I recently learned was a misdiagnosis." I had everyone's attention. "I have a multiple-personality disorder. Hana was hurt because I discontinued my medication. I thought I was stronger than my Dissociative Identity Disorder. I consulted my doctor in secrecy. It's very embarrassing not to feel normal or not to be looked upon as normal."

"Psychopathic isn't normal." The flabby Korean turned her flat lips into a grin.

Laughter tore through the crowd. Sade squeezed my hand. She made me feel confident that I was doing well. Her gestures proved to the cameras that she supported me. Exactly as we'd practiced it.

"I never meant for my condition to be the cause of Hana's hurt. I didn't ask to be like this."

✪✪✪

Hana and Shamar sat in front of a plasma screen watching Parrish's appeal to America. Parrish waved to the reporters, then he and Sade boarded the jet.

Hana clicked off the TV. "By this time tomorrow, I'll have more money than I'll know what to do with."

Don't count on it, Shamar thought.

✪✪✪

Tuesday slammed the pay phone on its cradle. "Fuck! Fuck! Fuck!"

"Everything will be all right," Silence said, looking at a dark congregation of rain clouds hovering over the city.

"No, Silence, it won't. His damn voice mail is picking up. I should have listened, believed him. I promised him that I would always protect him."

"For starters, the only thing you can do is calm down and leave Parrish a message."

✦✦✦

"Not at all," I said. "Whether I actually remember the incident or not, I'm taking full responsibility." My cell phone rang. When I saw that it was Tuesday, I turned on voice mail. Right now wasn't a good time for me to entertain people who didn't believe in me.

A slim black woman with pretty features stepped to the front of the crowd. "What motivated your decision to make a public statement?"

"Damage control. You guys made me look like an animal. I need everyone to hear my side, which will allow people to make a balanced opinion concerning me. In addition, this ordeal gave me the perfect opportunity to face myself and my illness. It's a tedious job living a lie."

"Two questions, Mr. Clovis." The flabby Korean again.

She was really beginning to get under my skin. "That's why we're here. Fire away."

"The woman you're sporting, who is she? And how do we know she won't become your second victim if you decide to have a mental hiccup while she's in your company?"

"This—"

"Let me." Sade faced the reporters. "I'm soon-to-be Mrs. Sade Clovis. Parrish ain't no threat to nobody. He's taking his medicine; he ain't no crazier than me and you."

Lightning flashed and thunder sounded off not two seconds behind it.

"That's my cue," I said, looking at the sky. "It's best that we get ourselves ahead of this storm."

"Where are you and Ms. Sade traveling to?" someone said.

That was the most important question, the only one I had come out to answer. "The International Film-makers Festival. I'm receiving an award this year."

❂❂❂

Three hours later, Sade and I were in Tampa, Florida, washing down red snapper fingers with mai tais and in the company of the festival's event coordinator.

❂❂❂

"Detective Duval Micheals speaking." He grit his teeth, thinking he would hear his wife's voice and be forced to navigate the rough terrain of her nagging. "Who is this?"

"Anonymous will do." Jeanette watched the ferry cross the Hudson.

He pumped his fists victoriously after ducking his wife. "I once read somewhere that someone made an artistic contribution using that name. What can I do for you?" He removed his pen cap.

"It's what I can do for you."

"Okay. Surprise me."

"There's a dead body at 427 Oak Street."

He jotted down the location. "And how would some-one named anonymous know that?"

"Wrong question, Detective." Jeanette walked to the end of the pier. "You have the body. Your interest should be on who murdered Mr. Ace Driscoll."

"Indulge my interest."

"Officer Shamar Lindsay." She wiped her fingerprints from the disposable phone and fed it to the swelling Hudson.

✪✪✪

When I heard the toilet flush, I whispered into the phone, "I have to go."

Sade came out of the bathroom as I folded my cell phone. "Who was that?"

"Nobody but my sister. She's meeting with Hana for dinner."

"You look flushed. You having second thoughts, ain't you?"

I reflected back on my phone conversation. "Not at all." Hana had to pay. I set the DVD player to repeat, hiked the volume, and started the porno flick.

Sade hung the *Do Not Disturb* sign on the knob. We could hear the TV-couple inside our room having sex.

"Perfect," Sade said.

✪✪✪

Hana gazed through the window at the night. "This storm is absolutely stubborn."

Tuesday turned to Silence. "We girls need to chat. Do you mind giving us a few minutes before we leave?"

Thunder boomed through New Jersey. The house's lights flickered.

"Take all the time you need," he said, pushing away from the table. "I'm in no rush to go out in this weather. I'm gonna hang out in the library with Rudy while you ladies talk. Maybe I can teach him to cuss in Spanish."

"Please don't," Hana said. "He'll practice on me. Whatever you do, don't touch him. He bites everyone but Parrish."

"I guess I'll have to bite him first."

Tuesday and Hana watched Silence leave.

"You've got yourself a trophy." Hana looked at her watch, 9:52 PM.

"Cut the bullshit. What the fuck do you want?"

Chapter 37

Everything had gone according to plan—so far. Sade and I were back in Jersey by ten pm. I thought the storm would put us behind schedule, but I was able to fly above it without a problem. By 10:13 PM., I was in my car about to drive out of the hangar.

Sade waved me to a stop. I lowered the window.

She said, "Be careful. Hurry back to me." She leaned in and planted one on my lips.

"Our lives will be different in forty-five minutes." I put my foot on the gas pedal.

✪✪✪

"Parrish keeps six million," Tuesday said, "the house, job, and salary."

"You're pushy for someone receiving a handout." Hana remained unreadable. She didn't allow her expressions to squeal.

"See, that's where we disagree. I can't prove anything; it's just my gut feeling that you've taken advantage of Parrish for financial gain. Categorically, this isn't a handout but a robbery."

"Silly girl," Hana said with a *tsk*, *tsk* while reading her watch. "Had I taken something I wasn't entitled to, I wouldn't return any of it."

"You're checking your watch like I'm keeping you from something important."

"My affairs aren't your concern. Do we have a deal or not?"

"Make the charges go away. Tell them you lied; that it was a burglar if you have to. Whatever you have to do, I don't care. Just make the charges disappear."

"Agreed." Hana listened to the rain bombard the house. "The paperwork will be prepared first thing in the morning. I'd appreciate it if you'd be my overnight guest. Come morning, I don't want to wait any longer than I must to be through with you or your brother."

Thunder sounded off. Seconds later, lightning knocked out the electricity for miles. The space between Hana and Tuesday went pitch black.

"You ladies all right?" Silence's voice was distant but approaching.

"I'm fine," Tuesday said as she felt his presence enter the room. "Looks like we're staying in the guest room tonight. Do you mind?" Her eyes adjusted.

Hana seemed nervous.

"It's cool with me." He put his arm around Tuesday as Rudy flew in.

"Dumb fuck," Rudy said.

"The guest room is mine. You two will have to occupy the master bedroom."

"We can't," Silence said as lightning briefly brightened the house. "That would be rude."

"What happened to me in there was horrible. I can't sleep in there."

Tuesday didn't like the idea of not being able to get a full visual of Hana's face. She wanted to compare Hana's expressions with her words.

"I must step out for a moment," Hana said. "Tuesday, your car is blocking mine in. Mind if I drive yours?"

❂❂❂

Clockwork. Sade smiled as the car with personalized *Tuesday* plates drove into the hangar. She climbed into the passenger's seat, and then hugged Hana. "All of those years of acting school are finally paying off. I hate my character's ghetto qualities and poor English, but this was the best script I've ever had. It's a shame I wasn't on film."

Hana put her foot on the gas pedal. "The pay off-screen is better than it is on-screen. Besides, it's not time to celebrate. Parrish still must squeeze the trigger."

"He's done it once; he hates you more than enough to do it again."

Chapter 38

T he sky was dark and quarrelsome, reflective of my mood. Lightning split the night sky in two. The heavens cried a steady downpour of tears. The heavens' choice of pain purging was tears. Mine? Double homicide.

✪✪✪

Shamar and Ball Game sat in an idling BMW. Shamar took a .357 from between the seats and handed it to him. "When Parrish realizes what happened, he might do your job himself. If not, Hana must be dead before my old buddies down at the station show up." He started driving toward Hana's. "Everything we've done will be wasted if she lives. Her greed will cause her to cross us out."

"You've been working to cross her from the start. You and your acting friends are a treacherous lot." Ball Game set the gun on Shamar's lap. "Up until now, I've followed your orders to the letter. Played dead and all. It's time for some answers. I'm no actor, but after spending all those days in a musty motel, all I could do was think. You wanna know what I came up with?"

"Not particularly."

"I have the most important role. Something goes wrong, I'm going to prison like everybody else. I'm not going back to the pen in the blind. You have a choice: tell me everything or murder Hana yourself."

Shamar needed Ball Game to perform. He took a breath and began to explain.

✪✪✪

"Hana, we shouldn't go there," Sade said as they drew nearer to First Born Lane. "I need to get back to Florida before someone realizes I'm not there. Shamar will handle it from here. We didn't rehearse this, nor did we leave room for improvising."

"I helped write the script; I'm well aware of what there's room for. Your pilot is waiting as we speak. In a couple of hours you'll be back in your hotel suite as planned. I need to hear the gunshots."

"I do not like this, emphasis on the *do not like*."

"Calm yourself."

"It's thundering and lightning. You can't hear anything if you wanted to."

"I beg to differ."

"Take me to the plane. Then, you go and listen all you want."

"You know how I am. There is no way I can watch;

hearing will be the only thing to satisfy me. We have thirty-two million riding on those shots."

The storm picked up. Sade's cell phone rang.

"Hello." Sade knew that they were making a huge mistake.

"Do what you do best—act," Jeanette said. "Hana cannot know that you're talking to me."

"Grandma, what are you doing awake at this time of evening?" Sade flashed Hana a smile when she glanced. "There's a thunderstorm here."

"Shamar figures Hana will double back to the house. She can't control her curiosity."

"You're right about that. Maybe Christmas-time, Grandma."

"Ball Game is going to take her out if she does. The idea is to pin Parrish with all the murders."

"She's fine, Grandma. In fact, I'm with Hana now." Sade nudged her. "She says hello. I'll see what I can do about convincing her to visit with me for Christmas."

Hana frowned and shook her head in the negative.

"Go straight to the plane I arranged for you. Shamar is more piggish than Hana. Give him the opportunity to subtract you from the equation, and he won't hesitate."

"Not tonight, Grandma. I'm in the middle of some-thing. I promise to call her tomorrow."

Hana turned onto her street.

"Call you back, Grandma." Sade hung up on Jeanette. "Girl, pull over!"

"For—"

"Pull over, dammit!" She pointed to an SUV stopped in the middle of the street. "That's Parrish."

❂❂❂

"A bunch of reject actors thought of this?" Ball Game asked as Shamar pressed on through the storm.

Shamar shrugged. "Without Parrish's medical history and the doctor and lawyer element, it would've never worked. We picked Parrish and Tuesday when they were in junior high. We took their father away from them when it was time and gave Parrish Hana. We even set up his girlfriend, Erienne, with a job in Africa to get her out of the picture. It was that or kill her."

The depth of the plot amazed Ball Game. "Parrish gets murdered at the scene of the crime by an ex-cop."

"Yours truly."

"His wife gains control of his money and all that he inherits from Tuesday. But his wife is now your wife."

"Manufactured his signature on their divorce papers. Our marriage was dated after their divorce."

"Devious. When she dies, you inherit thirty-two mil."

"All we had to do was let Parrish taste murder when he believed that he popped you. A few hours in the bedroom with Sade, she convinced him to do it again and that he could get away with it."

"A piece of ass that good could convince Jesus to murder. I'm a little messed up over her myself."

Shamar tapped his horn at an SUV blocking the street. "Hana cannot control that money."

Ball Game shoved the gun in his waistline. "It's no guarantee Hana'll show up."

"She's a nosey white girl. Her nature won't allow her not to." Shamar watched the SUV ease up Hana's driveway as he parked farther down the street. "Another thing: the less people involved, the richer we are."

"There's plenty to go around."

"Sade. She can only keep a secret if she's dead. You know what to do if you see her tonight." Shamar kept his eye on the SUV as it was being parked behind Hana's car.

Parrish climbed from behind the wheel and went inside the house.

✪✪✪

The sway of my windshield blades was hypnotizing, sedative even. They seemed to wipe the blur away from my vision. They seemed to wipe her ugliness away from my thoughts. The SUV's idling engine was smooth. Meditative. Healing.

Only a moment slipped by before *her* ugliness tormented me again.

My palms were slick with evidence of my nervousness. I gripped the steering wheel, thinking. I forced a fidgety foot to keep pressure on the brake. My worn-out brown eyes were fixated on the Italianate structure eleven yards ahead of me, a place that I was once proud to call home. Neighbors, passersby, and associates from our inner circle of influence considered this type of home a symbol of status, success. I, on the other hand, know that it represented four wasted years, failure, regret.

Everything beyond the handcrafted doors facing me, taunting me, was what I once loved. A love that was patient, kind...neither was it envious nor boastful—just love. I stored no records of wrong, not until she had taken off her mask and showed me her ugly face.

Now, everything beyond the threshold of those doors, beyond the security system, was everything I hated worse than my mother.

Lightning parted the night again; thunder barked behind it. Call me crazy, but it seemed as if the thunder were cussing me like I were a little boy in need of scolding.

My BlackBerry glowed; its ring tone crooned a neo-soul tune by Vivian somebody. The sultry lyrics reminded me of what I must do: *Gotta go, gotta leave.* I wished I could blend with the rain and trickle down in the sewer. I pressed Send but didn't bother to say anything. I wasn't in a talkative mood. I gave the caller nothing more than a deep breath.

✪✪✪

"He's always been such a wimp." Hana's nostrils flared. "He's backing out." She stopped the engine but left the air conditioner running to prevent the windows from fogging.

Sade stared at Parrish's brake lights. "What are you doing?" She spoke her thoughts out loud. She hit the autodial feature on her cell phone. The phone rang twice, and then she heard Parrish sigh. "Parrish, is you...everything okay?"

Although he didn't feel it, he said, "I'm fine."

"Twenty minutes is left before you hafta cross the Holland Tunnel and come to the airstrip. Then, we home free." She couldn't believe he was sitting in the middle of the street.

A bolt of lightning lit the sky.

Sade shrugged at Hana and raised her brows. "You there?"

"Wish I were there with you."

Why in the hell are you sitting there? "Is you sure you okay? Boy, you don't sound like it."

"I will be after tonight." He put his focus on the glove compartment.

"Where are you?" Not that she had to ask. "We gotta schedule to keep."

"Outside of my house...thinking."

"You done, then, ain't you?"

"No."

"No?"

"*No!*"

"Damn, boy, you 'bout to blow everything. You trippin'." She paused to collect herself. "Hana deserves this.

We done come this far; now ain't the time to be fuckin' thinkin'." She sighed. "You was s'posed to be done and on your way back to me. This plane gots to be in the sky before our cover is blown."

"Don't press me. I'm not in the mood. We'll make it."

"You scared. It ain't even difficult. Fuck that bitch."

He stared at the house.

"Stay right there. I'm on my way. I ain't scared. I'll do it my damn self."

"I said I'll take care of it."

A husky horn was blown. Hana and Sade knew the BMW well.

Parrish eased his foot from the brake. He shut off the headlights and parked in his driveway behind Hana's car. "Listen to me, Sade."

"Ain't I here?"

"I never want to feel this type of pain again. Every woman who's been in my life has hurt me. Promise me that it ends with you. I don't want to hurt anymore. I love—"

A burst of thunder covered his words.

"Boy, ain't I already done made that promise? How many times you wanna hear it? Keepin' it real, if I wasn't serious 'bout us, I wouldn't be mixed up in this bullshit with you. I woulda never aborted my baby for you. Love is a verb. Now is a good damn time to show me." She hung up and turned to Hana. "He's going to do it."

He removed the .9mm from the glove compartment.

The fox has many tricks, and the hedgehog has only one,
but it's the best of all.
—ERASMUS

Chapter 39

Silence could hear the rain pounding on the roof as he paced the dark bedroom. After what Tuesday had just told him, he started thinking of the conversations he'd once had with Ball Game, his old cell mate. The thoughts both scared him and made him angry.

"There's something I should tell you."

"It can wait, okay? It'll be all right," Tuesday said. "We'll pretend we're somewhere else. Your bed."

After what she had revealed to him, he really wished he had taken his chances with the weather. "This has to be the craziest... no, this *is*—"

"Trust me." She peeled her blouse off, exposing her breasts. She pressed her nipples against his chest while tasting his lips and undoing his belt.

***

The house was as quiet as it was dark. I knew my space well, however. My eyes adjusted to the absence of light; what I didn't have in vision, I compensated with memory. Lightning burst through the night. Its brief illumination highlighted the gun in my hand. My heart was banging so hard, I actually thought I was hearing it with my ears. I stood at the bottom of the staircase. Rudy was perched on the banister as if he were there to collect toll.

He said, "Asshole."

Asshole was all that he could think to say to me after being apart for weeks. Nevertheless, his blunt truth always seemed to amaze me. I felt like an asshole. I probably even looked like an asshole standing there with a gun. Then, I heard them making love. My squeaky bed was proof. I thumbed the safety off like a skilled marksman. For as long as I live, I'll never forget what Hana had put me through. And now it was time for her and Shamar to pay. I shooed Rudy away and started up the stairs. The closer I got, the louder the squeaks became.

I eased the door open.

"More. More," I heard her say just above a whisper.

I could only make out their thrusting images. She moaned each time he pushed into her. I raised the gun. Hana would never have the opportunity to hurt anyone again. I pulled the trigger, holding it tight until the gun coughed out the last bullet.

The squeaking stopped.

I rushed down the stairs and out into the rain.

Tuesday's Mercedes pulled into the driveway behind my car; its windshield blades in as much of a hurry as I was. I held my breath and never considered breathing again when I saw the person in the passenger's seat.

❂❂❂

On the North side of Hoboken, Jeanette heard the squawk of two-way radios filter in from somewhere behind her. The sound was as misplaced as a nude woman in a man's locker room. *Cops*. She drew on a cigar and focused on a golf ball that was patiently waiting near her feet to be abused. She gripped the golf club, cocked back, and then let it rip. The ball hauled ass down the driving range into the rainy night.

"Ms. Jeanette Daniels," a twenty-something rookie officer said. He tapped his equally novice partner; an indication to spread out and secure a physical perimeter around the perp. "Mind putting the club down, Ms. Daniels?"

By the way he had stumbled through the syllables of her name, and by the polite way in which she had been instructed to disarm herself, she had every reason to believe that this visit from Hoboken's finest was far removed from cordial. She gripped the golf club tighter. She faced him, boring her eyes into him with an intensity that was impossible to ignore.

"You were told to let go of the club, Ms. Daniels," Officer Leon Page said, unsnapping his holster.

Rookie gave Leon a slight nod. "Ms. Daniels, you're

under arrest for conspiracy to commit murder for financial gain."

She heaved her chest. She knew that someone would snitch in court. With the murders of Walter J. Clovis, Ace Driscoll, and Meaghan Broadwater being in the pot, she knew that she would spend the rest of her days behind lock and key once she was handcuffed. *If the federal prison system had golf courses, maybe it wouldn't be so bad.* She grunted.

Rookie reached for his gun.

Over her shoulder she heard Officer Page demanding that she release the golf club. Before Rookie could free his gun, she crashed the golf club into his wrist, crunching the bone with ease.

Officer Leon Page froze.

She gnawed on the smoldering cigar and swung the golf club with a powerful, sweeping motion. She abused Rookie's head harder than she had abused the golf ball she'd sent soaring beyond the 300-yard marker.

Rookie swallowed his last breath before he hit the ground.

"Put the fucking weapon down and get the hell away from my partner." Officer Page pointed his gun at Jeanette's thick back. "Do it now!" He began to unthaw.

She was calm, knowing that a gun was trained on her. For a long moment she watched how the blood oozed from Rookie's gash and puddled at her feet.

"Put it down or I will put *you* down." His words were well paced.

She raised her hands above her head; the left hand still clutching the golf club. She turned to Officer Page, cigar smoke clouding her vision of the young officer. It was like a sheet of smoke was suspended between them. She wondered if the way Leon Page appeared to her now was how people looked in heaven.

"My partner is in need of medical attention. You have no other alternative than jail. The longer it takes for me to apprehend you, the greater the risk of my partner dying. You don't want that on your hands." He pulled in a breath. "Release the weapon, turn around, drop to your knees, and place your fingers behind your head. Now!"

"There are other alternatives outside of jail. Jail isn't what's in my forecast." She put her right hand on the handle of the golf club. She held it above her head like an ax. "Tell me, Officer, have you ever wished you could be God? Come on, don't give me that look. We all have at some point, for some reason. To have the power over life and death has to feel great. Power. That's why you became a cop, right?"

He shifted his weight from one foot to the other. "Don't do this."

"You don't seem to understand. I want you to realize your wish of being God for a time, for you to have control of ultimate power. Even if the experience only lasts as long as it takes to squeeze the trigger. In doing so, I'll realize my wish of divine intervention." She drew hard on the cigar. "Always thought it'd be the cigars." She drew hard again and lunged forward.

Officer Page fired his gun. Baptism by gunfire.

❊❊❊

I wasn't sure which would defeat me first, the rain pounding on me or the sight of Hana living and breathing. She stood five feet away without so much as a scratch.

Grinning.

But the person staring from behind Tuesday's windshield distorted my view of human beings. I looked back at my bedroom window. My eyes swelled with water.

"Oops. Wrong person," Hana said.

"No, not my sister."

"It was designed that way. While your father was grooming you to receive his fortune, we were plotting to take it. That plan didn't consist of Tuesday being amongst the living."

I screamed the equivalent of the hurt I was feeling. I dropped to my knees. "Why? I loved you."

"You were kind to me. You love Erienne."

I balled my fists and shot them at the sky. "Why, Hana? Why did you do this?"

"Money is a mighty motivator. Walter made an abundance of it; we made certain that you and Tuesday inherited the funds much sooner than nature's clock."

I rammed my fists into the driveway, bawling.

"I permitted you to meet me when it was time for me to become your next of kin. You understand how enriching that position is for me now that Tuesday is no longer with us. Jeanette is an excellent attorney; the paperwork is orderly. We're not—"

"We? Who is we?" I looked through Tuesday's windshield. "Who else?"

"You saw the pictures of us all: Lucinda, Shamar, Jeanette, and me. We're all in your life by design." She fell into thought. "As I was saying; we're not cruel; we've created you a way out, Parrish—the whole memory loss, identity-disorder thing. It was all a ruse. Nevertheless, we're very good at what we do, Parrish. Your medical records will stand up against the scrutiny of medical experts and trial judges.

"All you have to do is walk through the door of opportunity we've extended you. You'll plead insanity and spend a few years in a mental hospital for criminals. Now that I'm your next of kin, and you aren't mentally competent to manage your financial affairs, I control your estate. I'll make certain you're well taken care of. Tuesday will also have the privilege of a decent burial. It's the least I can do."

"I would've given you anything you wanted." I was soaked to the bone. "Anything, Hana."

"Entirely not true. Had you given in to my pseudo fantasy, we would've taken this scheme in another direction. I counted on you to get angry and deny me. I require it all. Tuesday's share as well."

"You murdered her for it."

"You pulled the trigger. I only reaped the assets."

"I'm not going to keep quiet or plead insanity."

"You will keep this between us, just like you kept the truth about your mother's death a secret." She was overly confident. "You should really learn to watch your mouth when you're asleep."

I ignored her comment about my mother. "Somehow I signed it over to you. All you had to do was divorce me."

"You're such a silly man. That was only a backup plan. Something is better than nothing. My intention was never divorce. Your money alone is too small. The threat of divorce is what led us to where we are now. It's the reason I control it all."

"I won't help you."

She rubbed her belly. "She kicked yesterday. Her name is Paradise."

"Hana, I have such a terrible feeling about this," Sade said, stepping out the car. "We should never have come here. I really think we should be going."

"Look at me, dammit! What about the ultrasound pictures at our house?" I said to Sade.

"They're of our little girl," Hana said. "If you ever want to see her, you'll play along nice. I'll be the supportive wife while you're away, visit you and permit you the privilege of watching our daughter grow. Playing along is the only way you can be a part of her life."

It was hard for me to catch my breath. I found Sade's eyes. "And what about you?"

"Hana, please," Sade said.

Hana's laugh was more evil than before. "Her job was to encourage you to kill me."

"Hana, it's time to leave."

"Should have never come." Ball Game uttered those words and then shot Sade in the back of the head. He moved closer to us with Shamar not two steps behind him.

I winced when Sade hit the wet concrete. I looked up into Ball Game's face and knew I wasn't staring at a ghost.

"Sorry, Uncle." Ball Game spun toward Shamar with neck-breaking speed and let off two shots, hitting Shamar in the chest. He kneeled beside Shamar and removed his gun. "Hana pays better than you."

Shamar gasped for air; his body went into shock. Ball Game stood and pointed the gun at Shamar's head, hoping to finish Shamar off.

"Do it," Hana said, clearing a wet tress from her face.

"Wait!" I said, ripping my shirt open.

Ball Game glanced over a shoulder and saw the wire and microphone taped to my chest. Tuesday and Silence rushed from the house. Hana turned pale. An assortment of marked and unmarked police cars started toward us with urgency.

Silence and Ball Game locked gazes.

"Bitch!" Tuesday landed a solid fist to Hana's face, knocking her on her ass.

Beacon lights bounced off of the neighborhood. Several cops were yelling for Ball Game to drop his gun. Then, it happened. Ball Game fired three quick shots; each one hit me in my upper body. I had never been hit that hard by anything. Then, I heard a rapid succession of gunfire.

Tuesday and Silence were crouched beside me. I felt cold and wet. "I'll get an Oscar for that performance. You'll be best supporting actress." I was looking at Tuesday, but she was eleven years old again.

Tuesday nodded and sobbed. "I should have...believed you. I promised to always protect...you." She was sobbing uncontrollably. "I'm sorry, Parrish. Please...don't leave me."

Everything slowed down. I couldn't feel my fingertips, or maybe it was because the burning sensation in my chest overpowered all. I could see the rain falling, but I could no longer feel it. Their faces hovered over me. I had to warn her. "He—"

"Don't talk."

My vision blurred, but from the deep Southern drawl, I knew that Detective Duval Michaels had spoken those words.

"Hang in there, buddy," he said. "You're gonna be fine. The medics are coming." He pushed water from my face. "We missed the gunshots. The rain shorted your mike out. Mrs. Kaffka and Doctor Rodriquez are in custody. If Officer Lindsay lives, he'll spend the rest of his life in jail."

Tuesday was right beside me. Her sobbing, however, was distant and growing faint. I blinked Silence into focus. It took all the energy I had to say, "He's...a part... of this." My eyes closed involuntarily. Keeping them open was no longer an option.

Chapter 40

Tuesday cradled Parrish. "Please open your eyes, Parrish." She rocked him. "Who has something to do with this?" Then, the answer hit her. She looked at Silence; he lowered his head.

Duval picked up on the guilt etched in Silence's features. In one fluid motion, Duval had the deadly end of a gun directed at Silence.

Tuesday's voice went calm; her words were delivered slowly. "He's wrong, right?" Her lap cushioned Parrish's head. "Right?"

Silence remembered the day Ball Game was being released from prison. Ball Game had given him a folded piece of paper with a number written on it. He had told Silence that there was a legitimate job and apartment waiting on him. All Silence had to do was call. "It's true," Silence said, looking Tuesday square in the eyes. "I was involved without knowing it until tonight."

"You lying son of a bitch. You've been lying to me from go."

"Lay flat on the ground," Duval instructed. "Thread your fingers behind your head."

"All that positive thinking and you loving me was bullshit!"

The paramedics went to work on reviving Parrish. Duval carefully handcuffed Silence.

"I do love you, Tuesday. That's the truth."

"I trusted you, knowing I shouldn't have. You're just like everybody else."

Silence struggled to prevent Duval from getting him to his feet.

"Take it easy." Duval put his knee in Silence's back.

"Let me talk to her, then."

Tuesday nodded her head as the medics slid a gurney beneath Parrish.

"You got one minute." Duval drove his point home with a knee.

Silence grunted. "I swear I'm telling you the truth, Tuesday. I was set up, too. I didn't know for sure until we came out the house. I had an idea when you told me about you and Parrish's conversation and the plan. I tried to say something to you then, but you made me wait. When I saw Ball Game, it all clicked. He was my cellmate in prison. If you and Parrish hadn't figured out what Hana was up to, we'd both be dead.

"The gig at the driving range and the apartment, Ball Game lined it up for me. All I had to do was call Jeanette when I got out. I went to see her, Tuesday. The only way she'd give me the job was if I agreed to take you out. She told me that you'd be at the driving range on the third of September. She even told me that you'd come on to me; try to get me in bed. I figured a date in exchange for a job and a place to stay wasn't bad for an ex-con." He paused. "I didn't know that a date would lead me to be emotionally involved with you."

"You can finish explaining to her down at the station." Duval lifted him to his feet. Duval had heard many stories where criminals claimed to be innocent. The only thing different about this one was that he believed it.

"Listen to me, Tuesday. I love you. Tonight was the first time I've seen Ball Game since I've been out. Think about it; I was supposed to be in that bed with you. That's how they were going to cover their tracks on my end."

Duval ushered him into the backseat of a police cruiser.

Silence banged his head on the window until Tuesday looked in his direction. "I love you."

She removed several strands of hair from her face and climbed into the ambulance with Parrish. Before the door closed, she heard Silence ask her to believe in him. That was a request she didn't have to think about.

Epilogue

My eyes fluttered open in slow motion. My surroundings were brilliant white. Minutes seemed to pass between each blink. There was no sound, only white. The weird thing about this place was that was there were no doors or windows. Then it dawned on me. No, I can't be. Am...am...I dead? This setup wasn't exactly how I had imagined nonexistence. I was dead. Over. Kaput.

An instant peace embraced me as I realized that I was in a waiting room of sorts.

A white one.

I began to wonder if I would go through an interview process before being granted admittance to a place where I'd no longer be dangled between continuous states of confusion and make-believe. Suddenly, anxiety weighed me down. What if I didn't qualify to become a resident of eternal happiness? I closed my eyes and crammed in some prayers.

I hoped that, at this stage of death, my prayer account was still open. *Big Guy, I see You've made Your call. I'm not asking for You to reconsider and send me back. That, however, would be nice...I would keep my promise to my pops and look after Tuesday. I would tell Erienne what she means to me. I'd also teach Rudy some good words. Granted, I know my timing is a little late, but I'm asking that You extend Your mercy to me by sending me forward.*

"Parrish."

I stiffened. "Come on, Big Guy, I'm almost at the amen part."

A hand stroked my forehead. "I told these people your pain medication was too strong."

I looked up at Erienne's fuzzy image. I blinked my focus clear. Her smile was warm, wide, inviting, alive. *Big Guy, You work fast.*

"Thought I'd lost you," she said, tugging back the white curtain that surrounded my bed, opening my vision to a large hospital room with doors and windows.

"Kiss me." It was all I could think of to check my reality. I felt her soft lips press on my parched ones. "Again."

"That better?" she said after the second one.

I nodded, becoming aware of the tubes in my nose and the IV in my arm.

"Tuesday...where is she?"

"Near. You've been in and out of it for twelve days now. When the doctor released you from ICU and informed us that you'd be fine... She's in rehab getting herself together. She waited until two days ago to sign in. She's in love."

I smiled, and then frowned.

"I'll explain it to you later. Parrish, I need to apologize. I should have—"

"Shh. That's uncalled for. I understand."

She sat down in the chair beside my bed. "Where do we go from here?" She fell silent, staring at her lap. "I've looked for you in other men for as long as we've been apart. Every time I think I've found you, I wake up empty and the person beside me is everything you're not."

I thought about what I'd promised the Big Guy I'd do if given this chance. "I love you without a logical explanation as to how. Erienne, I don't even have a reference point to figure out where it all began. What I do grasp is that I've been loving you so long, I know no other method." Then, I thought back to what Pops had schooled me on when deciding on matters of the heart. "I don't want to change the water."

She intertwined her fingers with mine. It felt great.

"I brought someone to see you." She bent down farther than I was capable of seeing. She came up and set a portable bird cage in the chair and started fumbling with its door.

"Don't. He'll bite the feeling from you."

"He's a sweetheart," she said, removing him from the cage. "Rudy and I have an understanding."

"I've never seen anyone able to handle him."

"That's because animals can pick up on good and bad vibrations. Everyone that you witnessed try to fool with him was giving off bad vibes." She set him on the bed railing.

He and I considered each other for an undetermined time.

"Dumb fuck."

Erienne and I laughed.

I rubbed his feathers. "Not anymore, Rudy."

"Not anymore, not anymore," he said, stretching his wings.

Author's Exit

Wow! Here I am. It's a funny situation, though, because sometimes you don't know how close you are to success until you seriously contemplate giving up. For me, it's the inspiring smiles, encouraging whispers, and unspoken expectations of the people who believe in me that keeps me keeping on when giving up is much easier. Hands down, it is because of the following amazing souls that I woke up this morning and found myself living my dream, cruising down its path.

Eunice Whitmore, Grandma, you're no longer with us, but I carry you in my thoughts, words, and deeds. As a little boy you taught me the moral imperative of finding my purpose and of gifting it to the world. I found it, Grandma. I'm doing like you told me. Thank you for being a gift to me. I love you.

Eric, Rashaad, and Rasheed, my cool-ass sons, you guys changed my life. Your presence is a humbling experience. Thank you for having unrelenting belief in me. Listen: our separation is drawing to a close; we'll never be apart again. So get ready, because once again, it's on!

JaVenna Smith, my twin flame. You are proof that

dreams come true. Your existence is why my soul is no longer in search of its mate. Thank you for being a part of my whole, the yin of my yang. 619—always!

Silence, my little-big brother. The words I truly need to express my appreciation for you haven't been created yet. Man, you believed in me before I was even sure if I truly believed. You knew that today would be a reality long before anyone else. Thank you for all of your encouragement and support along the way.

Docuversion, my editors, thank you for the great work you've done on *Duplicity*. You guys are truly the vanguard of book editors.

Brenda Hampton, my friend first, then my literary agent. My question to you is, where do we go from here? I trust your guidance; I'm feeling the way you instinctively got my back. You are a great person. Thank you for all that you have been, all that you are, and all that we will become together.

Tina Brooks McKinney, you spoke this into existence as well—my marriage to the majors. In fact, you tried to hook up the first date. Tina, I appreciate you for so many things, but I want to specifically thank you for blessing me with your friendship.

Charmaine Parker, Publishing Director of Strebor Books, thanks for your vote. Without your stamp of approval, I wouldn't be down with the team.

Zane, thank you for giving me a shot and for welcoming me into the folds of Strebor. This opportunity means a lot to me; it's the introduction to my future in this game. All I can do from here is show and prove.

Okay, don't trip. If there is anyone I failed to mention for their contribution to *Duplicity*, charge it to my absent-mindedness and not my intentions. We all know that this book wouldn't be possible without you.

Oasis
Oxford, Wisconsin
June 2010
oasisreader@oasisnovels.com

About the Author

Oasis is a craft expert and certified creative writing instructor. He is the author of *Duplicity* and *Push Comes to Shove* and the CEO of Docuversion, a full-service editing firm. His next novel, co-authored with Mrs. Oasis, is *White Heat*. To learn more, visit him at OasisNovels.com.

IF YOU ENJOYED "DUPLICITY," BE SURE TO CHECK OUT

Push
COMES TO
SHOVE

BY OASIS

AVAILABLE FROM STREBOR BOOKS

PROLOGUE

Greg Patterson hung in the nude from a vaulted ceiling by his young wrists. His 110-pound body was no match against the leather restraints. He wriggled and rocked himself past the brink of exhaustion. There was nothing else he could do now but wait.

He'd lost track of time, hanging there in the cold dark. He wanted to relieve himself, but pissing on Mr. Reynolds's floor wasn't an option. It would only make matters worse.

Footsteps fell in the hall right outside of the door. Greg hated this part with passion, but at least...at least it was almost over.

The tarnished doorknob spun left.

He braced himself.

The group home's disciplinarian, Mr. Reynolds, stood in the entrance with a bucket of sudsy water in one hand. His widespread body covered the majority of the doorjamb. "You refuse to learn your lesson."

"I won't steal again. This time I...I promise." He gestured *no* with worry.

"Foolhardy boy, you've made that meaningless promise since you learned how to talk." He dowsed the frail boy with the sudsy water. "A little incentive will keep you focused. You should really keep your hands off things that don't belong to you." He wrapped the ends of a heavy-duty extension cord around his bone-colored hand. "You'll learn one way or the other."

"Mr. Reynolds, please don't beat me this time." Greg clamped his burning eyes shut, hoping the soap would stay out. "I needed the art supplies for school. Untie me and...and I'll take them back right now."

"After I give you an ass cutting for being a habitual rule violator." He hiked his gravy-stained sleeves past his pudgy elbows and stood behind the boy.

Greg tensed, anticipating the first blow.

Mr. Reynolds raised his arm and swung the cord with a batter's determination. "If I could beat the color off of you, I would."

The cord sounded like thunder when it cracked against Greg's brown skin.

"Aargh…no more! I'm sorry, Mr. Reynolds." Greg stiffened all over. "Please, no more. I won't do it again. I'm sorry."

"You *are* sorry, aren't you?"

The cord slapped him once more, this time breaking the skin on his back.

"You're a piece of stinky shit, and that's all you'll ever be is shit."

Thunder struck again.

Greg yelled out so loud, he threatened to short out his vocal box.

"You're a bum, Greg." He switched hands and swung from a different approach. "That's all you'll ever be. Why do you think you've been here all these years? Nobody wants a bum; not even your mother."

Mr. Reynolds had lashed Greg until his arm was tired. He went into the hall and looked at his aged yes-man. "Untie him. Lock the thieving bastard up until his wounds heal. And get rid of those drawings he's always wasting time on."

"Right away, Mr. Reynolds."

CHAPTER 1

GP decided that tonight his family would eat good for a change. He eased the Renault Alliance to the order box; it stuttered and backfired every inch of the way.

"Welcome to Wendy's. May I take your order?"

He shut the car off so that he could hear. "Excuse me... uh, could you run that by me again?" He could hear the cashier suck her teeth through the speaker, as if she was annoyed.

"Good evening, how may I help you?"

"Gimme six number sevens with large fries...and extra cheese. Make the sodas orange, no ice." He thought about how Kitchie loved Dave's chicken. "Uh, let me get two spicy chicken sandwiches and four baked potatoes with cheese. I guess that'll be cool."

"Would you like to try our apple turnovers this evening?"

Fuck it. "Yeah, why not? Gimme six and six large chocolate Frosties." He waited a few seconds for her response.

"That'll be forty-eight twenty-three at the pickup window. Thank you for choosing Wendy's."

GP tried to start the Renault. "Come on, baby, crank

up for Daddy." The engine strained but wouldn't catch. He pumped the gas and rubbed the dashboard. "Come on, girl. I need you now more than ever."

He turned the key again. The engine backfired, then came to life. With three vehicles in front of GP, his order would be ready in a matter of minutes.

His car sounded like a Harley Davidson outside of the pickup window. An attractive cashier rolled her cat-like eyes and shook her head. *Derelict*. She turned her lip up with attitude as she passed him three large bags and two drink-holder trays.

"That's forty-eight twenty-three." She smirked and stared at GP.

GP secured the drinks on the front passenger seat, then stomped the gas pedal. The Renault backfired.

The cashier all but jumped out of her skin.

With the power-steering pump broken, it was a difficult task for GP to make the sharp left turn. He jerked and tugged the rebellious steering wheel until he yanked the car onto Euclid Avenue.

He stuck a fry in his mouth and smiled. GP knew that, on this April Fool's Day, he would be the cause of three beautiful smiles.

Four city blocks away from his home, the Renault had had enough. The engine light came on right before the car stalled.

"Come on, baby, I thought you loved me." He coasted to the curb. He tried to restart the engine but it refused; it only made a clicking sound.

If he started his journey on foot now, he would make it home long before the food was cold. With a bag between his teeth and two in his hand, he reached for the door handle but hesitated when he saw a Cleveland police car pull up behind him.

"Fuck me!" he mumbled, then lowered the window with a pair of vise grips. *Damn cashier could've let me slide. Ignorant chickenhead didn't have to call the cops.*

§ § §

Miles dropped his skateboard on the sidewalk, then stepped on it with an Air Force 1 sneaker.

A fragile image appeared in a screen door behind him. "Miles...Miles, baby, you hear me?"

He removed the headphones from his ears as his broken arm remained at rest in a sling.

"Miles, baby?"

"Huh?" He turned toward the house as his mother walked out onto the porch.

"See if you can find your brother. It's dark. I'm starting to worry; this isn't like him." She adjusted the belt of her housecoat and folded her arms.

"Jap is probably somewhere standing next to a tree, testing his camouflage gear. Better yet, he might be with one of his weird friends on some type of mock-military scavenger hunt."

"I'm serious. Don't tell me what you think; do like you were told. We have to get a fitting on him in the morning for his graduation gown and cap, and I want him home."

"Okay, Ma. I'll check a few places on my way to work." He started off on the skateboard.

"Miles, baby …"

He stopped and faced her again. "If you don't let me go, I won't have enough time to check on Jap and make it to work on time."

She removed a prescription slip from her housecoat. "Drop this off at the drugstore, and I'll pick it up in the morning. I'm getting low on my heart pills."

He hurried up the steps, took the slip, and kissed her cheek. "See you later, Ma."

She grabbed a hold of his cast. "Why don't you get yourself a car? You can't afford to get too many broken arms on that thing."

He followed her gaze. "I love my board, Ma. I'm gonna ride until I'm an old man."

"You're still a baby to me; you ain't considered young no more."

§ §§

The officer surveyed the car and shined his flashlight toward the back seat. "What seems to be the problem tonight, sir?"

GP had replaced the large order on the front passenger seat. "Damn thing conked out on me. Four cylinders are supposed to run forever."

The officer looked at the beat-up car from front to rear. "What year is this?"

"It's an eighty-five." GP was starting to feel comfortable.

"Twenty years old *is* forever for a car." He pointed at the Wendy's bags. "Looks like you're going to be late for dinner."

"Yeah, I'm pushing it."

"Well, you can't leave it here overnight." He shined his beam on a *No Parking* sign. "It'll be towed by morning…which is probably the best thing for it."

"This is all I got."

"Come on; let me help you push your headache to that lot." He pointed.

The officer wiped his dusty hands on a hanky after they had rolled the car onto the lot. "Wendy's doesn't sound like a bad idea."

"Not at all. Thank you, officer." GP pointed his feet in the direction of home.

§ § §

Kitchie Marie Patterson glared at GP through a set of powerful brown eyes. "Let's talk…in the bedroom." She led the way.

GP shut the door behind himself. "Before you start, Mami, I only wanted to do something nice for you and the kids."

"There's at least fifty dollars' worth of food in there,

GP. You stole it, didn't you?" She shook her head with disappointment.

"You and the kids deserve the world." He stroked her almond cheek; she turned her face away. "I can't give it to you right now, but one day I will. Until then it frustrates me to want y'all to have things that are beyond my reach."

"Then get a job—a real job. You don't have to quit your hustle but get a job, GP. How far do you think we can get on your hopes and dreams alone? This is the real world we're living in; not some animated world like them cartoon characters you're banking our future on." She thought for a few seconds. "Now you're to the point of stealing again. Yeah, you made the kids happy tonight and saved me the humiliation of throwing some bullshit together, but what's gonna happen to their happiness—" She pointed toward the living room. "—when you get yourself in some trouble?"

"You act like I steal for the sport of it, Kitchie. I steal for one reason: because *we* really need something, and I have no other alternative of getting it. I felt like we *needed* to sit down tonight and share a decent meal with each other, like a regular family."

"A real nine-to-five will make that possible every night, Papi Chulo."

He heard something else in Spanish that he didn't quite understand, but understood she was trying to take this conversation to a place he wasn't willing to go.

"Listen…my work is honest; it's what I love to do. I don't want to go back and forth with you. This isn't what I intended. All I want to do is see your beautiful smile as much as I can." He lifted her chin with a finger. "Let's eat. The food is getting cold. I got your favorite."

She bit her bottom lip. "Chicken?"

"Dave's spicy chicken sandwich. Now let me suck on them Puerto Rican lips of yours."

She stood on her tiptoes to reach his six-foot height, then kissed him on the mouth. "I wish you would shave and get your hair braided; it looks like you gave up." She pulled back. "GP, you can't keep stealing whenever it's convenient for you. One day stealing is gonna get you in some trouble you're gonna catch hell getting out of."

"Or get me out of some trouble I'm already catching hell with."

§ § §

Greg Jr. took a bite from the double classic. His seven-year-old teeth barely plugged the cheeseburger. "Daddy, I need my own bike. Secret's bike is hot pink with that stupid, flowered basket on the handlebars. Everybody makes fun of me when I ride it."

Secret was trying her damnedest to suck the Frosty through a straw. She gave her jaws a break. "Stay off my bike, then, since it's stupid and pink, punk. I don't like sharing it with you anyway, you little—"

"Hey, kill the name-calling." Kitchie stopped chewing and frowned at Secret.

"Little man." GP squeezed Greg Jr.'s shoulder. "Bear with me; I'm gonna get you the best bike in the neighbor—"

"Don't be doing that, GP. It ain't right." Kitchie swallowed her food. "Okay, fine, tell him you're gonna get him a bike. But don't be making these fantastic promises that you can't deliver. You're doing terrible in the delivery department. Don't do him like that."

"How many times do I gotta ask you not to challenge me in front of the kids?" He wiped the corners of his mouth with a napkin. "When you feel like I said something that should be corrected, talk to me behind closed doors."

"We can still hear y'all in the bedroom arguing." Secret kicked Greg Jr.'s shin.

"Ouch." He tried to kick back but his legs were too short to reach her under the table. "Ma, tell her—"

"Stop, Secret, and quit being so damn grown." Kitchie focused on GP again. "I apologize, Papi...I'm a little frustrated; that's all. I still don't want you to get Junior's hopes up only to let him down. That'll hurt him more than getting made fun of."

GP finished the last of his burger. "There's nothing wrong with hoping, having faith in something; especially when I know that I can make it happen." He looked at his family one by one. "Let's get this out in the open so we all know. Secret, what do you want? What does my baby's heart desire?"

"Hmmm…I can say anything I want?"

"As long as it's appropriate coming from a nine-year-old." Kitchie sipped her soda between bites.

Secret's expression was thoughtful. "Daddy, I want my own room." She rolled her eyes at Junior. "Lots of new clothes like my friends would be nice, too. Oh yeah! I want a puppy, and I hope you give me my piggy bank money back that you borrowed last month."

GP stroked the top of Junior's head. "And what about you?"

"All I want is a bike, but I'd take a PlayStation if what we're saying is real."

"What about you, Mami Chula?" GP blew Kitchie a kiss. "Tell me what you dream of when you close your eyes."

"This is pointless. I'm not getting involved with this… stuff." She started on her apple turnover.

"Aw, Ma." Secret sucked her teeth. "Tell us; we wanna know."

"Yeah, it's only a game." Junior dropped a French fry in his lap. "We're playing pretend."

Five seconds passed and GP leaned forward. "We're all waiting." He was unsettled by his son's comment.

"This is foolish, GP, and you know it. If it must be known, what I want more than anything in this world is for my marriage to defy time." She began to blush, then the reality of their current situation hit her. "I want us to have a bigger house—bought and paid for. I'm not big on having a lot of money, but I wish we could at least be comfortable and able to send you guys to college when it's time."

"Your turn, Daddy." Junior balanced his chair on two legs.

"The first thing I want is to be in a position to give y'all everything you want. And I want to always be able to protect y'all from danger. Comfortable might be cool for your mother, but I need our bank account to be sitting on at least a million. Of course, I want the Street Prophet to get recognition on a national level, a Saturday morning cartoon or something."

"Take the French fry out your nose, boy, before it gets stuck." The look Kitchie cast across the table put Junior right in line.

Someone knocked at the door.

"I'll get it." Secret pushed away from the table.

Kitchie grabbed her by the pants. "Make sure you know who—"

"It is before I open the door." Secret finished Kitchie's sentence. Secret stood in front of the door. "Who is it?"

"Publishers Clearing House Sweepstakes," came from the other side of the oak.

Secret pulled the door open as far as the chain lock would allow. She studied both white men in their jeans and button-down shirts.

One had a clipboard with a large envelope fastened to it.

"Where's the microphones and TV cameras?"

The bigger of the two men laughed. "That's only for our grand prize winners. Third place doesn't get that type of publicity. Is Kitchie Patterson in?"

"Yes, would you hold on a minute?" She freed the chain lock and ran into the kitchen. "Mom, Dad, you're never gonna believe who's at the door. The Publishers Clearing House people. Ma, you won."

Kitchie looked at the ceiling. "*Gracias Dios.*"

The Patterson family rushed into their living room.

The smaller, balding man was unplugging their TV from the wall outlet.

The other man thrust the envelope toward Kitchie. "Your Rent-A-Center bill is overdue. You've been ducking us for over a month now. We're here to collect or repossess." He turned to his coworker. "Set that down and go around the corner and get the van."

"Don't you people have an ounce of feelings?" GP stepped between Kitchie and the envelope.

"Sometimes it's an ugly job, but it pays my bills. If you would tighten up on your payments, I wouldn't even be here." He slid the envelope under GP's armpit. "Straighten out this five-hundred twenty-three dollar bill and I'm out of here."

GP sighed. "I don't have it right now." He heard Mr. Reynolds's antagonizing voice in his head loud and clear. *You're a bum, Greg. That's all you'll ever be.*

"Then I'll start with the kitchen set and work my way through here." He pointed to the furnishings.

§ § §

The Patterson family watched through a window as the two men loaded the last of their furniture into the van. Kitchie fought to hold back the tears.

The bigger man came back inside with sweat beads on his temples. "Mrs., I'm sorry. Would you please sign here?" He passed her the clipboard and put his finger on the spot where he wanted her signature. "Would it be possible for me to trouble you for a glass of water?"

GP stared at the man as if he had asked for blood.

"Junior, get the man something to drink." She scribbled her name on the form.

Moments later, Junior returned with a tall glass of water.

The man drained the glass. "Ahh, now that was good and cold." He turned and left.

Kitchie surveyed their bare living room. Secret was sitting on the radiator, finishing her meal. So much for having a decent meal like a normal family. She went and stood beside GP at the window. "Publishers *fucking* Clearing House. They cleared us out all right." She and GP watched the Rent-A-Center van drive away. "Papi, this ain't an April Fool's joke. You need to do something. This is only a prelude to what's next."

GP dropped his head and heard Mr. Reynolds shouting at him for what had to be the millionth time. *You're a worthless piece of shit. Your mother should have swallowed you.*

Kitchie walked away. "Maybe a glass of cold water will calm my nerves." She turned on the faucet to fill her glass. The water was lukewarm. She checked the refrigerator. No water jug. No ice. "Junior!" She put her hands on her round hips. "Where did you get the cold water from?"

He looked at Secret and they laughed. "Promise you won't get mad, Ma."

She returned to the empty living room, hands still on her hips. "Boy, what did you do?"

"Everybody knows the coldest water in the house is in the toilet."

CHAPTER 2

The morning sun cast its strong rays through the living room. Secret sat in the middle of the floor with her lip poked out and arms crossed. "Why can't I stay home and go to work with you and Ma?"

GP tied his worn-down boots. "Because school is important. You don't take days off just because." He yelled upstairs. "Kitchie, you and Junior get it together. If we're not out this door in the next five minutes, the kids will miss the school bus, and we'll miss our bus, too." He went and sat down beside Secret on the floor. "The only time you don't want to go to school is when you have to ride the bus. Is someone bullying you?"

"Yeah, right! You should be asking if I'm bullying somebody. How soon before you get the car fixed this time?"

"I'm not sure if it can stand another fixing." He straightened her collar. "Secret, when did you start keeping secrets from me? If you don't talk to me, I can't help you."

She sighed. "It's these two girls—sisters—Tameka and Kesha Stevens. Everything is about money with them. They be bragging and showing off because they was in

Bow Wow's video. I only see them at the bus stop and that's when they shine on me. They think they're so special because their father is a bank president. National City this, National City Bank that. They be having the hottest stuff, and I gotta go to school in this." She ran a hand over her skirt. "I got this last year, and I got this shirt on my seventh birthday. They don't forget nothing; they make sure everybody else remembers, too." She sucked her teeth and lowered her head. "When you drop us off at school, I never see them because our grades are different."

"Secret, some people are blessed more than others."

"Does that mean they have to be mean and embarrass me because they are?"

"No. Some people are ignorant and don't know it." He put his arm around her neck. "What do you be doing while they're…broadcasting their ignorance?"

"Shoot, I be getting smart right back."

"But you're the one with bruised feelings in the end."

She looked down at the floor. "Seems that way."

"Being made to feel small or embarrassed isn't fun. People shine on me, too, when they can. I don't like it at all, but I learned something."

She looked at him with wonder.

"I found out that people will keep running their mouths as long as you fuel them with a response. Your mother and I are raising you to be tough, right?"

"What does tough have to do with it? I can beat them both, if they don't jump me."

"Tough goes beyond being physical, Secret. If you're tough enough to ignore them, they'll leave you alone and find someone else to bother. Someone they can get a response from."

Kitchie sauntered into the room with calculated grace, holding Junior's hand. "Let's go."

GP helped Secret up. "Would you ignore them for me today?"

"I guess." She threw her backpack over a shoulder. "Try and get the car fixed fast."

"I'll try. Promise that you'll be tough until I do."

"I promise."

§ §§

"Daddy, there they go right there." Secret rolled her hazel eyes. "The two with the Cartier shades and Gucci sneakers."

GP did a quick examination of the two little girls across the street. He had to admit that the sisters looked like a million bucks. He kissed Secret's forehead. "Don't sweat it. Remember what I told you." He gave Junior a high-five and whispered in his ear. "Hold your sister down."

The children kissed their mother, then headed across the street.

"Secret, hold your brother's hand." Kitchie thought about how much things had changed from the time her children were toddlers.

The folding hydraulic door hissed open as the Rapid Transit Authority bus halted in front of GP and Kitchie. They gathered their belongings and climbed onto the bus.

"Good morning." Kitchie flashed a bus pass and gasped. "Did you see that?" She pointed a manicured finger toward something outside the window.

The driver followed the direction of her index finger. With a sleight of hand, she slipped GP the bus pass.

"See what, lady?" The driver turned back.

"That man over there almost got hit by a car." She went and took a seat.

GP climbed the last step, flashed the pass, then sat beside Kitchie.

❈ ❈ ❈

By noon the hustle and bustle of downtown Cleveland was in full swing. Vendors of all varieties had their booths lining the sidewalk between East Fourth and East Eleventh Street off Euclid Avenue.

Kitchie's part of the hustle was powered by two sources: undue beauty and charm. She was a people magnet. No man could resist the urge to regard her almond hue stretched with precision over a five-foot, four-inch frame accessorized with a tiny waistline, firm breasts, and a thirty-four-inch curve that stuffed the backside of her jeans. Whenever she tossed her nut-brown hair and smiled, Kitchie would reel them in every time.

"Do you have this for a toddler?" Suzette Sanders held up a Street Prophet sweatshirt.

"We don't stock that particular item in children's sizes. But my husband can custom-make you one." Kitchie noticed a man standing near the costume shop's display window, and his blue eyes were undressing her. "If you give me your child's size and a way to reach you, I'll have it ready for you in a week."

"That'll be fine." Suzette dug a business card and pen from her purse. "The choice is yours. I'm a volunteer at the mission two blocks over."

"I know the place."

"I'm there every day until around this time." She finished writing on the back of the card. "You can stop by there or call me, and I'll come by and pick it up."

Kitchie took in the information on the card. "Real estate."

"In my spare time. The majority of my time is spent trying to leave the world better than I found it."

"I'll give you a call. I can remember this number by heart, prefix all fives." Kitchie shoved the card in her back pocket as Suzette strolled away.

Blue Eyes was still watching.

Kitchie rested both hands on her hips. "You can't get a proper look from over there." She flashed her admirer a smile. "Come closer so you can really see what I'm working with."

Blue Eyes stepped away from the costume shop positioned in front of her booth. "If I knew it was that easy, I would've come over here twenty minutes ago."

"Well, now that you realize it wasn't as difficult as you thought, let me help you make up your mind on what you should buy from me." She tossed her hair away from her face. "Now you wanna be the first to get this, because when the Street Prophet goes global, you wanna be able to say you were down with the Prophet from day one." She held a T-shirt up to Blue Eyes and saw GP approaching with a struck-out look etched on his face. "You look like an extra large. T-shirts are ten a pop, but for you…I'll give you two for fifteen." She tossed her hair again and tucked a lock behind her ear. "And I'll throw in some Street Prophet stickers for the kids." She looked at GP in his Street Prophet shirt and air-brushed jeans. "There goes a loyal supporter of the Prophet."

Blue Eyes glanced at GP with contempt, then focused on Kitchie again. "I'm not interested in any of your Street Prophet merchandise. What *does* interest me is your number and a dinner date to discuss my e-zine endeavor."

"Forgive me, but it's a rule of mine not to give out my number on the first purchase. So what'll it be, two for fifteen?"

He laughed. "Sexiness and persistence. I like." He peeled

off a twenty-dollar bill. "Where is that adorable girl I've seen around here a few times?"

"My daughter? Why?"

"I thought we could discuss this over dinner. I'm in the process of launching an internet magazine, and I'd love to use your daughter as a model in an issue or two. She's beautiful; you two look just alike."

"Thank you. When you're ready, come back and my husband and I will see what you have and consider it."

"Keep the change." Blue Eyes took the shirts and blended into the sidewalk traffic.

Kitchie stuffed the money in her pocket and rose up on her toes to kiss GP. "What did they say?"

He began setting up the airbrushing equipment. "We can't get another extension. The bank's attorney said if I come up with the principal, penalty charges, and his fees, he'll stop the foreclosure proceedings. Other than that, foreclosure is final and we have five days to be out."

Kitchie pulled the bill from her pocket. "I've been standing out here all morning and this is what I made." She waved the money. "Papi, you tried but this ain't panning out." She motioned to the Street Prophet items around the booth. "I know your dream is to give this character a life; I've supported you in everything. It's time to give it up because these twenty dollars can't pay our bills. We're past the point of do-or-die." She scrutinized the money closer. "*Vete pal carajo!*" She turned in the direction that she'd last seen Blue Eyes.

"What's the matter, Mami?"

"That bastard burned me." She passed GP a dollar bill with the corners of twenties glued over the numeral one.

A Korean woman hung the pay phone up next to GP's booth and it soon began ringing. She went to answer it.

"Excuse me, ma'am; that's for me." GP stepped away from the tables, unconsciously glanced at the street sign, then lifted the phone from its cradle. "Ninth Street Artwork, home of the Street Prophet. How may I help you today?"

"May I speak with Greg Patterson?"

"He's in the art room with a customer. Can I tell him who's calling?"

"Tracy Morgan. I'm an acquisitions editor for the *Plain Dealer*."

"Hold on a minute, I'll get him." GP covered the phone and gave Kitchie a thumbs-up.

A local bum strolled up with a cup in hand. "Spare some change, GP?"

He shoved Blue Eye's pseudo-twenty into the cup, then placed the phone on his ear. "Greg speaking."

"Good afternoon, Mr. Patterson. I'm Tracy Morgan with the *Plain Dealer*. You filled out an application with us some time ago. Sorry I'm just getting back with you."

"It's cool. What's up?"

"Your sample work has impressed quite a few people in my department. If you're still interested, I'd like to interview you. I have a comic column available that I believe you'll do great in."

GP wanted to say hell yeah; instead he chose to keep things professional. "I'm interested. When would you like to meet?"

§ § §

Kitchie had worked pedestrians moseying the sidewalk; GP had solicited various motorists who had been delayed by a stoplight near the booth's curb. At the end of the day, they had earned a little over ninety dollars, which barely covered the booth's weekly rental fee.

Due tomorrow.

"I sure hope they give you that column. It'll help out a lot; plus it'll get your foot in the door." Kitchie cleared a table, stuffing merchandise inside a duffle bag.

"Keep your fingers crossed." He packed the airbrushing guns.

A 2005 Chrysler 300C with mirror-tinted windows stopped at the red light near the booth. The car wasn't moving, but the chrome rims appeared to continue spinning.

The window was lowered.

"The starving artist who thinks he's gonna draw his way to financial freedom." Squeeze looked past GP and studied Kitchie's round ass. "Long time no see."

GP squatted some and leaned on the passenger door

of the Chrysler. A gorgeous woman sat there, snuggled with a dozen roses. GP nodded at the woman, then addressed Squeeze. "It's been a while. What's up with it, Squeeze?" He admired the man's diamond-studded pinky ring. "I see you stepped it up a few notches from knocking over candy stores. What is it, you poison people for a living now?"

Kitchie was now standing beside GP, caressing his shoulder.

"I'll be the first to tell you that crime pays the bills. Candy stores were just a stepping stone, though. I'm the neighborhood loan officer now. Got fucked-up credit but need some cash? Holler at your boy." He stared at Kitchie's crotch, pulled her pants down with his eyes, and had his way with her. When he was done, he turned his attention back to GP. "I see you still holding on to all that woman. I never could figure out why she chose you. I must not have been square enough."

"Don't act like I'm not sitting here," the woman holding the roses said.

Squeeze hit her with a backhand across the mouth. "Stay in your place."

A car horn sounded off. Squeeze ignored it and pulled out a business card. "Don't be bashful; if you ever need a loan, I'm sure I can work it out for an old friend." He gave GP the card, then took a long-stem rose from his date's bundle. "Give this to Kitchie. I'm sure you haven't bought her any in a while." He winked at Kitchie.

The window was raised and Squeeze sped away.

"God, I can't stand him." Kitchie took the rose from GP and dropped it in the curbside drain.

§ § §

"What are you gonna tell Mom and Dad?" Junior squashed a caterpillar that was crawling on the porch steps.

"Shoot, that I had to kick her butt. She put her hands on me first." Secret watched her brother scrape the bug from the bottom of his shoe. "You think Daddy will ever get us all that stuff we named last night?"

Junior ran the question through his head, then shrugged his shoulders. "I don't know...Nah, not all of it."

"Go in the house and get us something to drink."

"I ain't; you go."

Secret nudged him. "Scaredy-cat, you're too old to be afraid of the dark."

"I'm not thirsty. Go get your own drink."

"Chicken."

"You must be scared yourself."

She smirked. "No, I'm not."

"Go get something to drink, then, with your ugly—"

Kitchie pointed to the light pole while coming up the driveway. "What did I tell y'all hardheaded butts about being outside when them street lights are on?"

"It's lighter out here than it is in there." Secret aimed a thumb toward the house.

Junior skipped to Kitchie. "Something's wrong with the lights. They broke, Ma."

Kitchie sat the duffle bag down, looked at the dark interior of their home, and began to cry.

§ § §

GP climbed a steep hill that led to Cliffview Apartments. He never understood why they were called apartments when they ranked as no more than drug-infested projects.

He went into the building and held his breath to avoid inhaling the thick cocaine smoke as he passed a group of addicts smoking crack on the stairwell. He reached the third floor and pound on his best friend's door.

"Don't be banging on my shit unless you're in a hurry to get fucked up." The metal door squealed as Jewels yanked it open. "Oh, what's up, homeboy? I thought you were somebody coming to borrow some shit. A motherfucker asked me to borrow my dustpan yesterday."

Their fists touched in a greeting manner.

"I did come bumming."

Jewels turned away from the door. "You don't count."

She wore brush waves and dressed better than any man GP had ever known. Beneath today's expensive urban wear was an average-looking woman. She was built like Serena Williams but much stronger.

She lay back on the weight bench and pumped 225 pounds effortlessly. "I didn't hear that raggedy-ass car of yours pull in the lot doing the beat box." She racked the iron after ten reps.

"You got jokes. It broke down yesterday. I went to check on it before I came here, but it was gone." GP plopped down on the designer couch in front of a McFadden and Whitehead album cover littered with marijuana.

Jewels sat up and stuffed a rolling paper with marijuana while looking at him from the corner of her gray eyes.

He shrugged. "I had to leave it in Chang's Chinese Food parking lot. Ignorant-ass Chang said it sat there too long, called my bucket an eyesore. Fake chink could've left my ride alone, you know?"

Jewels nodded and put a flame to the joint.

GP kicked a foot up on the coffee table. "He had it towed. Damn thing ain't worth more than it'll cost to get it out the impound and fixed."

"That's fucked up. Anything is better than footing it...unless you enjoy a good walk." She passed GP the joint. "Chang do got more Black in him than me and you, fronting like he grew up in China."

"Rent-A-Center stuck me up yesterday. I got five days to pay the bank or the foreclosure is final." He choked on the smoke, then released it. "And the list goes on. Junior wants a bike—which he deserves. Secret needs, and wants, new clothes to keep up with the Joneses. She's a good kid, too."

"You need some money, homeboy. It's cool to have big dreams and shit." She tugged at his Street Prophet shirt. "But you got a good wife and kids, too. They don't deserve to get dragged through a mud puddle while you chase your rainbow." She averted her gaze to her kick-boxing trophies lining the top of the entertainment center. "It's not about you no more, GP. You need to come up or do something to start contributing to your social security. Do your cartoons on the side. Fool, you ain't young no more; you got real responsibilities."

"Twenty-seven ain't old."

"It's too old to be dead broke." She pointed the remote at the flat screen. "You lucky I ain't never been on dick. If I had been the one to give you some pussy, for real, I'd do something vicious to you if you didn't take care of me and mine right." Jewels pulled out a nice-size bank roll. "How much you need?"

"I didn't come over here for money. I'll ask if I need it."

"You the one who said you came bumming. What your foolish ass want, then?"

"I have an interview tomorrow at the *Plain Dealer*. I need to borrow something to wear."

"Get out of here." She made a huge fist and tapped his chin. "Greg Patterson, Senior, a job interview? Hell must be below zero. Not only can you borrow something, you don't ever have to bring it back." Jewels led him to her immaculate bedroom.

§ §§